Randall Lane

A

Christmas

Spirit

A Christmas Spirit

by

Randall Lane

A Christmas Spirit

A NOVELLA
A Christmas Spirit
RANDALL LANE

"Oh my goodness!!! I just finished Devil's Den. What a roller coaster of a ride!!! I LOVED this book!! I can't wait to read your other stories, thanks again!!" — **Sherrie W Review for Devil's Den**

"This book was a real joy to read. Kept me turning pages well into the night. I just had to see what was going to happen next. This writer really has a way of drawing you into the story with subtle but potent descriptions that really set the stage for the story. And his characters really leapt off the page at you. They are so real and relatable, you can't help but like and cheer for them. This author is really talented, and I recommend you give his work a try. He makes it feel like you are right there in the story. It's like watching a movie. 5 stars for sure!!" — **Amazon review for Night Terrors**

"This is not a book that I would have normally read, but I went to a reading by the author and was mesmerized by his incredible skill at drawing you in with sensational detail. I was right there in the story and was spellbound by this affecting and powerful book! The writing is excellent, the story is compelling, and the book has a message that touches your soul, one you will not forget! Looking forward to more from Randall Lane! I give the Devil's Den five big stars!" — **Janet B Review for Devil's Den**

"I loved Devil's Den. It was scary and quite intense as I read through it. I could not figure out, "who dun it." I really enjoy a book that has me guessing until the very end. I can't wait until your next novel is published! Thanks for such an enjoyable read." — **Sandra N Review for Devil's Den**

"Wow! Where do I even start? I came across this book while searching through amazon for something new to read. The cover and title immediately grabbed my attention. I am so glad I purchased this book. I was instantly hooked on the first page and devoured the book within just a few days, and I'm even a sort of a slow reader. Could not put this thing down. I love the way the story is woven together, the characters were easy to connect with and root for, and the suspense was top notch. I had to keep reminding myself this was fiction. The way the author crafted the story made it feel so real. Definitely five stars from me and will be reading everything this guy puts out. Going to have to check out his other books also. Do yourself a big favor and give this author a try. I'm sure glad I did." — **Clyde S Amazon review for Devil's Den**

"I recommend this book highly. Devils Den. Can't put it down!"—**Marybeth L Review for Devil's Den**

"Awesome read! Once you start it's hard to put down! The way he tells the story keeps you captivated throughout the entire book." —Tammy P Review for Devil's Den

"I really enjoyed this book. The plot grew with an intense "who dun it" while surprising me with a twist I didn't anticipate. It's a great read in good vs. evil. You will find yourself questioning the validity of each character." — Happy Amazon Customer's Review for Devil's Den

"Mr. Lane writes with the eloquence of a storyteller. Deep, profound and superbly imaginative." — **Mark M Review for Devil's Den**

"Loved loved loved this book! Each story was unique, intriguing, and creepy. I really enjoyed the scary settings and all the different characters fighting their way through the darkness. Highly recommend this book and author. Well done! You've definitely gained yourself a fan! Keep it up!" — **Steve S Amazon Review for Whispering Winds**

"This author's imagination will leave you spellbound! These stories will excite your senses, give you pause to think and excite your very soul! Can't wait for more!!!!" — **Happy Amazon Customer's Review for When Darkness Hides**

"I WILL GIVE YOU A NEW HEART AND PUT A NEW SPIRIT WITHIN YOU; I WILL TAKE THE HEART OF STONE OUT OF YOUR FLESH AND GIVE YOU A HEART OF FLESH."

EZEKIEL 36:26

1

Monday
December 4th

The day slips away as Caitlynn Richards

crosses over the bridge and enters downtown Yawnoc. The town is decorated with lights and Christmas trees to celebrate the season of giving. People in long coats with their hands tucked under their armpits meander along the sidewalks amidst gazing into the storefront windows of all the little shops. Caitlynn watches their breath steam into the air. She comes to a redlight and bumps down her turn signal. As she waits for the light to change, she busies herself with tuning through the radio stations in search of good Christmas music other than just some cheesy cover of Jingle Bells or the like. A horse driven carriage full of people sipping on hot cocoa passes through the intersection. A little boy, with rosy cheeks and a red scarf, waves at everyone as if he were in a parade. Caitlynn chuckles at the sight. She pauses her turning of the radio dial when she hears Frank Sinatra's voice. Being an old soul at heart, she can't help but feel a little giddy when she hears singers from the days of old. As Sinatra sings *The Christmas Song*, the light turns green, and Caitlynn makes her turn. The horse carriage with the rosy cheeked little boy is up ahead. Church bells chime in the distance to ring in the four o'clock hour. Caitlynn reaches to the cup holder next to her right leg and takes hold of her coffee thermos. Three creams and two sugars equals perfection. She savors every drop as she feels its warmth. The bookstore comes into view. All the parking spots out front are taken as she expected they would be. She cuts down 8th avenue and finds a spot in the First Citizens Bank parking area. She gets out and begins her trek to the bookstore to pick up a new release from one of her favorite authors. Anthony Gerald. He usually writes mystery and sometimes horror type books but had surprised everyone with a Christmas themed ghost story this year. Caitlynn could hardly wait to cap off her day with picking up her new copy. It'd been a rough day at school as she has a sinking feeling she may have failed her biology 265 exam. God knows she could use a good end to her day. Especially after what she'd learned from her mother that morning. The words she'd never thought she'd hear emit from her mother's mouth.

Divorce.

Looking back on it now, she probably should've seen it coming. Not that her parents fought or screamed at one another, but she could tell they had lost the spark. She had heard from one of her English classes that the opposite of love isn't hate. It's apathy. A lukewarmness. Thinking of her parents' relationship now, that's the two words that flash before her mind. What would life be like with the two cornerstones of her life separated? God, what would Christmas be like this year?

With her mind lost in these thoughts, she is too slow to react to the homeless man stumbling backwards into her path. She crashes into him and sends the older gentleman crashing to the pavement in front of Ned's Diner. Caitlynn almost joins him, but her young age allows her to keep her balance. The acrid odor of urine, sweat, and hard liquor flood the air. The man had a white beard and mustache with white curls billowing out from beneath an orange hunter's wool beanie. He wore a checkered blue and black flannel with a ragged black trench coat. His cotton gloves were missing the fingers and calloused flesh emitted through the holes.

"Oh, my goodness. Are you okay?" Caitlynn says as she kneels next to the man.

His tattered cardboard sign lies next to him. People sneer as they walk past them. They've become nothing more than a boulder in this stream of busyness. Caitlynn feels the glares but couldn't care less.

The man grunts as he focuses his attention to his knee. "Aww, God. Oh, dang that hurt. Right on the old knee cap." He says while rubbing at it.

Caitlynn notices how rotten his teeth are. The ones that are still there that is.

"You think you can stand?" She asks.

The man winces and grumbles something under his breath. Caitlynn feels more eyes on them and looks to her left to find people seated against the window of Ned's Diner glaring and pointing. Some even seem to laugh at the two of them. Caitlynn wrinkles her nose and gives them a *What are you looking at* gesture. They turn their eyes back to their meals.

The old man begins to try and stand.

"Here, let me help you." Caitlynn says as she takes hold of his arm and guides him. "Are you okay?"

He enters a fit of deep, raspy coughs and nods his head. He lowers his hand from his mouth and says, "I'll be fine. I've suffered worse."

"Are you hungry? Do you need anything?"

He coughs into his hand again and shakes his head, "I'm fine honey. You've already been kinder than most. Most kids your age would've yelled and kept walking. I'm sorry for tripping you up. Guess I should watch where I'm going, huh?"

"It was just an honest mistake. I was lost in my thoughts. I should've been paying more attention."

He gives her a soft grin and turns to pick up his sign. He places a hand to the small of his back and grimaces. Caitlynn steps past him and picks it up to save him the trip.

She holds it in front of her and reads it for the first time.

Homeless Veteran. Anything helps. Willing to work. God Bless.

Caitlynn closes her eyes, sighs, and shakes her head.

"You're a veteran?"

"Yes ma'am. Served in the army for seven years. Fought and almost died like a lot of my friends in Vietnam."

"What in the world are you doing out here?"

She watches him swallow hard as if he had a sore throat. He shakes his head while looking at his feet and says, "It's a long story."

Caitlynn bites the inside of her lip and turns her attention back to Ned's Diner. She catches the people seated at the window staring before diverting their eyes.

"Can you wait here for just a moment?"

"Ma'am, you really don't need to do anything. I've already caused you enough trouble for one day."

She waves him off and says, "Wait right here, okay?"

He chews on his bottom lip and nods.

Caitlynn goes inside.

A bell above the door chimed as she entered. Chatter and Christmas music fill the space. The strong aroma of baked pastries and fresh coffee hangs in the air. An elderly lady and a teenage boy tend the counter. Another middle-aged lady with auburn hair makes her rounds to the tables, filling coffee, giving out tabs, and taking new orders.

Caitlynn glances over to the three men seated at the window, but they won't even look at her. She strides up to the counter and orders a large cup of coffee with a ham and cheese sandwich and a cream cheese filled croissant. The teenage boy rings up her order and Caitlynn steps back to wait. She looks outside to see the old man hugging himself and glaring up to the darkening sky. Though it never snows in Yawnoc, the clouds sure look pregnant with it today.

Moments later, her order number is called. Caitlynn gathers it and heads for the exit. She smiles and nods at the three men in the window as she walks out.

"Here you go, Sir. I wish I could do more."

She watches as tears begin to well in his eyes. His bottom lip trembles. He swallows and looks up at Caitlynn. His sharp blue eyes remind her of Paul Newman's. She watches a tear leak down his cheek.

Caitlynn has one trickle down her own.

"I don't know what to say. This is the nicest thing anyone has done for me in a long time." He says after sniffling and wiping his nose with the sleeve of his coat.

Caitlynn sniffles herself, clears her throat, and says, "Well, you deserve it. Thank you for your service." She pats his shoulder, and even with the heavy jacket, it was like touching a skeleton.

The man puts his head down and begins to cry.

Caitlynn moves closer and wraps her arms around him. He was hesitant at first. Like a beaten dog afraid to trust their new owner. The man eventually hugged her back.

After a moment, he pulls away from her and wipes his eyes.

"I'm Caitlynn by the way." She says while extending her hand.

The man switches the bag and coffee to his left and says, "I'm Phil."

"It's nice to meet you Phil. Where do you stay at night?"

Phil snorts and looks out into the busy street. A man and woman pass between them. Phil was saying something, but Caitlynn missed the beginning of it as it was overtaken by the words of the passing couple.

"—nights, I'm over by the park. If it's real cold, sometimes I go to the soup kitchen, and they'll let me stay in the lobby."

"It's pretty cold out now, do you think that's where you'll be tonight?"

Phil nods, "Most likely."

"I tell you what. I'm going to get some things together for you tonight when I get home, and I'll bring it to the soup kitchen in the morning before I go to school. Will you be there around seven?"

"I should be, God willing. But like I say, you're being too kind. You really don't need to be worrying about an old feller like me."

"So, seven it is?"

Phil smiles and says, "You're a stubborn one, aren't ya?"

Caitlynn chuckles and rubs the side of his arm, "I'll see you in the morning, Phil."

He breathes deep, tightens his lips, and nods.

Caitlynn steps back and returns to her trek to the bookstore just a few blocks away. The whole way there she couldn't get Phil out of her mind. She keeps seeing those steely blue eyes, that toothless grin, and white beard. He could be someone's grandpa. The thought of her own grandpa sleeping out in the cold like that sent a pang through her heart. As she reached the building of the bookstore, she turned to look for Phil in front of Ned's Diner. A sea of people passed to and fro, but Phil was nowhere to be seen. Caitlynn said a little prayer for him and turned her eyes back to the bookstore. As she did so, her phone buzzed in her coat pocket. She looks at the screen to see *Grand Strand Oncology*. She swallows the knot in her throat and stares at the screen, unable to answer in fear of what the news may be. She misses the call. Caitlynn raises her vision and sees a ghostly vision of herself in the glass door of the bookstore. Her scarf is crooked from the tumble and her long, curly blonde hair rests in front of the right shoulder of her black peacoat. She thinks how much she favors her mom just now. The sting of guilt fills her spirit for not having told her parents of the issues she's been having. And with the news this morning from her mom, it seems they have their own problems as well.

She adjusts her scarf and enters the bookstore.

2

Seated in his office behind his cherry oak desk, is Eli Grindall. He hammers out the last of an email, scolding a colleague and lecturing on their incompetence. Eli grinds his molars as he mouth's out the words forming beneath his fingers. He finishes the body of the email and clicks *send* without giving it another thought. He pushes away from the desk, huffs out a breath, and pinches his tear ducts.

A set of knuckles wrap on his door.

"What?" He asks in a not so friendly tone.

"The fax from Bloomington just came through."

Eli curses and adds, "Oh geez. Why couldn't it have waited till tomorrow?"

The young secretary proceeds to his desk and drops the file next to his computer.

"Mr. Grindall, you don't look so well. Are you feeling okay? You seem pale."

He snarls his nose and waves her off. "I'm fine Mandy. Don't you have something better to do than worrying about me?" He says with a sneer.

Mandy takes his words in stride and wrinkles her brows before crossing back to the doorframe.

"All I'm saying, is maybe you should go home and get some rest. It's been a long week, and it seems to be wearing on you."

Eli only growls a response as he focuses his attention on the file before him. He watches Mandy disappear from his peripheral. He reads and then re-reads the big bold letters on the fax. *SEE YOU IN COURT LITTLE FELLA!*

Eli bawls his fist so tight his nails dig into his palms, causing them to bleed. His jowls quiver as hot breath steams from his nostrils. Eli can feel his neck and face flushing with the rising blood pressure. He growls a curse and balls the papers up before shoving them into his mouth. He bites down on them so hard it hurts his teeth. Eli chews the papers then spits them out onto his desk. A crooked grin stretches his lips and in his raging fury, he begins to chuckle. Not from joy, but from one of those *sometimes all you can do is laugh* type moments. He calls the folks at Bloomington a string of curse words, then turns off his desk top monitor and rises from his chair. The top of his head takes a pounding from a ghostly hammer. Eli feels his pulse thump strong. He winces with each *Wa-Whump-Wa-Whump-Wa-Whump.* His mind fuzzes over and the room spins for a moment. He has to steady himself with a hand atop the corner of his desk.

When will this mess ever end? Eli thinks to himself.

He retrieves his coat, and decides he'll make a quick coffee run before retreating to the office for another long night of working through the lawsuit and looking over the financials in hopes for ways to stay in the green. Emily would be upset that he'll miss another dinner with her and Samuel, but he's got do what he's got to do. She should know that by now.

He crosses over to the window looking out to a grove of pines. The wind tickles the limbs and sends a pine comb tumbling to the earth. Dark skies creep closer in the distance. A chubby sparrow with his feathers all fluffed out lights on branch and bobs gently with the wind. Eli watches it fly away. If only he could do the same.

He closes the blinds and leaves his office.

As he marches down the hallway between his employee's offices, most which are vacant at this time of the evening, he sees Mitchel typing away at his desk. The pudgy man, with a black beard and glasses, looks at Eli and gives a soft smile. Eli doesn't return the gesture but only quickens his pace for the exit.

The young, attractive accountant, Catherine, rounds the corner, and he watches her eyes light up when she sees him coming. She has a folder in hand and holds it high while saying, "Oh perfect! I was just heading to your office. Hey, where are you going in such a hurry?"

Eli holds up his index finger and shakes his head.

It doesn't derail her. Catherine matches his stride and follows along side him. "The numbers are not looking good, Mr. Grindall. I know there is a lot of notes receivable out there, and I'm even factoring that in, but as you'll see—"

"Catherine, not now. Okay? I know things are bad. You don't have to remind me. I'm going to comb over the books tonight when I get back to my office. I have some ideas, but right now I need some coffee."

"Ooh, me too. Care if I join you?"

Eli grumbles and gives her a side glance, "As a matter of fact, I do, Catherine. I need some alone time, okay? Rain check?"

He watches a shadow pass over her face. His words were a bit sharper than he intended. Their venom no doubt had seeped into her heart after the sting of his tongue. She swallows and licks her lips.

"Next time, okay? I just need some space."

Catherine nods, "Sure. Next time then. And here, take this with you. You'll want to look it over later when you have time."

Eli grinds his teeth and takes the folder. He reaches the door, places an arm on the bar and looks back at Catherine standing a few feet away with her arms crossed and a scolded look in her eye. Eli tightens his lips and sighs before pushing through the door and stepping out onto the street.

A bitter wind bites his cheeks. Traffic passes him by. Someone blows their horn. Eli enters the stream of people on the sidewalk and makes his way towards Ned's Diner.

The sun is dipping behind the tree line and gives the Christmas lights in the streets more glow. As Eli continues on, his phone begins to ring. Must be Emily. He retrieves and finds he was right.

She doesn't give him a chance to say hello. As soon as he picks up, she's already asking, "Where are you?"

Eli sighs as he marches up to the corner of the street. He presses the crosswalk button and waits.

"It's going to be another late night at the office, Emily. There's nothing I can do."

Emily goes silent on the other end.

The lights change and Eli enters the pedestrian walkway. An elderly couple are in front of him. The husband is in a wheelchair and the wife walks with a cane. Rather than stop and ask if the old man wanted a push, Eli walks past them without giving it much of a thought.

"I just need some time to sort things out, that's all."

Emily doesn't answer.

"Are you there?"

He hears her clear her throat before saying, "I'm here, Eli, but the problem is . . . you're not."

"I'm sorry, okay. Things will get better. I promise."

"You've been saying that for years now."

He feels her words sting something deep within. He clinches his jaw and snarls his nose, searching for a comeback.

Before he can respond Emily says, "I guess it really shouldn't matter if you're here for dinner or not because truth be told, you're never really here even when you are. You're always dazing into the distance, thinking about the office. Thinking about work. Maybe you should take a mattress and pillow with you tomorrow."

Fire runs up his neck and he finds himself balling up his fists again. "Emily, I'm doing all I can here—"

His words are cut short when a smelly, old homeless man steps into his path at the last moment, causing Eli to crash into him.

"Hey! Watch where you're going, you stupid idiot." Eli belts.

The man had bright blue eyes with a white beard and a black trench coat. He held a cardboard sign saying something about being a homeless veteran and anything helps. The man stares deep into Eli's eyes, searching and prodding. Eli feels something move within him. He swallows a gulp and shakes his head.

The man finally diverts those sharp eyes and lowers his head. He turns and steps in behind a crowd of people going the opposite direction.

"What happened?"

Eli hears Emily's voice.

"Uh. Nothing. Nothing. Just stumbled into some homeless man. Anyway, as I was saying—"

"Save it. I've heard enough. Tomorrow, we need to talk."

Eli lets out a deep breath through his nostrils. Ned's Diner is just ahead.

"Okay. Tomorrow it is. I'll mark my calendar," Eli says with a sarcastic tone. "Tell Sam goodnight for me. Emily?" He pulls the phone from his ear.

She had already ended the call.

3

With her first class not starting until nine the next morning, Caitlynn planned to swing by the soup kitchen around sevenish like she'd told Phil, so she could drop off a bag of supplies to him. She had stayed late at the library to study for her zoology 201 exam which would take place at ten after her English 210 course. Her parents had already turned in for the night when she arrived home. She found her dad asleep on the couch with the television flashing sports highlights on his back. He had slept on the couch for the past month or so now seemed. It broke her heart to see her parents' marriage crumbling right before her eyes, and sometimes as silly as it seemed, she blamed herself for its impending collapse. Even while attending community college full time and working part time at a local veterinary clinic, Caitlynn felt it wasn't enough. She did her best to help with things around the house, and pitched in on what bills she could manage to help with, but she still felt like a free loader. It bothered her more and more each day, and especially now that her parents' relationship was in jeopardy.

She frowns at the sight of her father on the couch and does her best to ease the door shut behind her. She watches as he shifts a leg and mumbles something but not much else. Caitlynn takes the blanket that'd fallen to the floor and covers him up. She kisses his head before making her way to her room. Once there, she pulls out a backpack from her closet and fills it with canned foods and snacks she had bought from the store on her way home. She also made sure to add in socks, underwear, flannel pajamas, and a few extra long sleeve shirts. She sat the bag next to her door so as not to forget it in the morning.

Caitlynn retired for the night and tried to drift to sleep, but it was hard to do with a million thoughts rushing through her head. A sense of dread filled her spirit when the thought of that missed call from the doctor flashed before her mind. They had left a voicemail, but she didn't have the courage to check it. She thought about her parents. She wouldn't dare be the bearer of bad news. Not at a time like this. Especially with Christmas just around the corner. On the other hand, she felt guilty for not telling them. A sense of dirtiness wafted over her for wanting to hide her recent health scares from them. She would tell them, just not now.

Questions from her zoology exam study guide linger in her mind, before being overtaken with the image of those striking blue eyes of Phil from the street. What was he doing right now? Had he made it to the soup kitchen like he said? Was he stuck out in the cold? She clinches her eyes tight and says a little prayer for him. Warm tears leak down her cheeks and soak into her pillow. She sighs out a breath and eventually, after much tossing and turning, she falls into that black abyss like we all do.

†††

Tuesday
December 5th
THE NEXT MORNING Caitlynn finds herself pulling into the parking lot of the soup kitchen. Only one car is there. It's an older, white Toyota Camry. Caitlynn parks two spaces over from it. She takes up the backpack from her passenger seat and heads for the entrance.

"Whew. My goodness," Caitlynn says as she walks against the brisk wind biting at her face. She clutches the bag tight to her chest and marches onward. She tries the door, but it's locked as she figured it would be. She slides into a strap on the bag and cups her hands around the dark glass of the window. She can't see much, but it seems empty.

A voice from behind startles her. Caitlynn spins around.

"—till eight, Miss. You're a little early."

It was an elderly black lady dressed in a thick coat, scarf, gloves, and glasses. She had a sweet smile about her and gave off a grandmotherly spirit.

"I'm sorry. I didn't mean to startle you," the lady says with kind eyes and a gentle grin. She walks with a cane and waddles a little with each step. Her knees seem to ache under her weight.

"No. No, you're fine. I was just going to drop something off to someone. He's an elderly man who goes by Phil. Do you know him?"

The lady pauses at the base of the steps and thinks for a moment, searching the skies for an answer. Finally, "I can't say that I do, Sweetie."

"Really? He said he stays here sometimes when it's cold outside. He has a white beard and white curly hair. Said he was a Vietnam veteran."

Caitlynn watches the old lady tighten her lips and shake her head, "Honey, there are a million Phil's like that out there. You lose track after a while. Why don't you come inside where it's warm. I'll make you a cup of coffee, hmm?"

"No, that's okay. I don't want to impose. I really should be going, I guess."

"Oh, nonsense. Besides, I'm sure someone could use those supplies you have there. C'mon, let's get out of the cold." The old lady says before trying to climb the steps.

Caitlynn sits the bag down and goes to help her. She takes her by the arm and guides her to the door.

"My name's Caitlynn. What's yours?"

"Nice to meet ya Caitlynn. Name's Cecillia, but most people just call me Grandma Cilla. Make's no difference to me, I respond to both." She grunts out the last of the words as she conquers the final step. She digs into her coat pocket and retrieves a ring of keys. They enter and a wall of warm air greets them.

Cecillia flips on the light switch by the door. The room resembles a reception area at a hospital. An oval desk with two computer monitors, and a bunch of seats scattered about. Three long rectangular tables line the far-left wall. Boxes of plastic silverware and napkins sit at one end. Two large, white coolers sit on the floor of the same end.

"I bet you stay pretty busy this time of year, don't you?"

Cecillia steps behind the desk and says with a chuckle, "Busy would be an understatement."

"How many helpers do you have?"

"Not near enough, unfortunately. It seems like the number of helpers is always on a downward slope, but the amount of mouths to feed is ever increasing."

Caitlynn takes in her words and turns to look at the tables. She envisions lines of people holding plates in front of them. She can hear their chatter, smell their warn out clothes, and see the smile on their faces when they take their first bites of a warm meal.

She turns back to Cecillia, "What do I need to do to get started volunteering?"

Grandma Cecillia looks up from behind the desk and smiles. "You have a good heart child."

4

Over at the Grindall's home, Eli has just sat down at the breakfast table next to his son Samuel who is busy spooning up bites of Fruity Pebbles. Emily finishes pouring creamer into her coffee and brings a plate with a bagel and sliced orange to the table. Eli has a bagel and sliced apple on his.

Eli chews on his first bite as his mind sorts through all the chaos taking place at work. For starters, those jerks over at Bloomington are in for a rude awakening if they think they can just bully him around and disrespect him like that. He can't wait to see their faces when Sean Walters walks into the courthouse with him. He'll really stick it to him. If Eli can afford to hire him that is. Which is why the sagging financials have really been weighing on him as of late. Walters is the best there is in this field, and Eli has to do whatever necessary to hire the man, regardless of how much his retainer is. Even if it means taking out title loans. He'd rather do that and win the case than to be sued into bankruptcy by those sorry douche bags at Bloomington. He has to find a way to afford the man. By any means necessary. That man is his last hope.

Eli hears Emily ask Samuel, "Have you told Daddy what you asked from Santa for Christmas this year?"

Samuel dazes into his bowl of cereal and shakes his head.

Eli wrinkles his brows and looks at Emily.

She smiles and takes a sip of her coffee.

Eli clears his throat and asks Samuel, "What did you ask for, Son?" A moment passes, "Go on now. You can tell me."

Samuel swallows a spoonful of cereal and says, "I asked Santa for a puppy this year."

Eli huffs out a breath and pushes back from the table. He glares at Emily seated across from him as he sucks on his teeth and runs his tongue over them.

Emily grins and shrugs her shoulders.

"No. We're not having any animals. They're nasty and a waste of money."

"But what if Santa—" Samuel started to protest.

Eli raises a finger and says, "Ah ah ah. No buts. Not under my roof. You can have a farm when you're grown for all I care. There will be no animals in this house. Period."

"Eli." Emily says with her head tilted to him.

"I don't care. You start with one and pretty soon it'll be a circus. The answer's no."

Emily shakes her head at him in disgust.

Eli ignores her and pretty soon is lost in his thoughts. His mind goes back to the day his dad shot his Husky for killing his grandma's cat when he was about the same age as Samuel. He always says in his mind that his dad shot his dog, but it was Eli who pulled the trigger. His dad had helped him hold the gun and forced him to pull the trigger despite his tears and screaming. Afterwards he received a good lashing from his father's belt and was given a lecture on being more responsible. That was the last pet Eli ever had. Eli doesn't have many memories of his father as he was a disciplined businessman like Eli himself and was hardly ever at home. That one memory though will stick with him forever.

Emilly's voice pulls him back.

"What did you say?" Eli asks after clearing his throat.

"Geeze, you're like talking to a robot. You know that? I said, there's a tree lighting tomorrow evening in Yawnoc I'd like us to go to. They light up the star at seven. We can go after supper. Grab some hot chocolate while we're out? What do you say?" Emily says, exchanging glances between him and Samuel. The way she looks at Eli makes him feel she's daring him to say no. As much as he'd like to and spend those precious hours at the office, his wife's look just won't allow it. He gives in and nods. Not without already planning to retreat to the office when they're finished.

5

After finishing the exam and reading the questions and checking her answers for a second time, Caitlynn has gained the courage to gather her things and head down front to turn in her work to the professor. About one third of the class had already turned in their tests and left the room. One of those students was her friend, Alexandria. Caitlynn drew a deep breath and held it as she approached the professor's desk. The old man was busy reading a C.J. Box novel. Looked like one about that game warden Box often writes about. There may have even been a show based on it. A plethora of random thoughts continue to flash before her mind as she gently places the exam, face down, onto the old professor's desk. He glances up from the novel, smiles, and gives her a wink of encouragement. Caitlyn smiles back and whispers *Thank you.*

She makes her way out the door to find Alexandria with her back to the wall and her nose in her phone. She looks up when she hears Caitlynn coming.

"That wasn't too bad, was it?" Alexandria asks with a wince.

Caitlynn shakes her head, "No, I feel better about that one than I do the biology exam. At least I didn't have to guess as much with this one."

"Yeah, same here. The study guide Mr. Bishop gave us really helped."

"No kidding. That was a life saver."

They continue to chat and walk alongside each other as they head for the parking lot. Stepping outside, Alexandria undoes her ponytail and lets her long, black hair drape over a shoulder before asking, "Hey, you want to grab some lunch before math class?"

"Sorry, I've already committed to lunch with Mom. You know how we have lunch together once a month. Today's the day. I would say you're welcome to join, but we do sort of need it this time."

"Oh no. No. I totally understand. I'm glad you and your mom and working things out. You don't have to explain anything, girl."

"Thanks," Caitlynn says as she pinches Alexandria's arm. "Maybe tomorrow? I picked up a shift at the clinic, but I could take lunch around twelve thirty or so."

"Tomorrow would be perfect. It's a plan."

With that, the two hug and go their separate ways.

Moments later, Caitlynn finds herself pulling into First Citizen's Bank parking lot before making the walk towards Ned's Diner. She's thirty minutes early, but she doesn't mind. With her copy of Anthony Gerald's new book in tow, it'd give her a chance to knock out a few chapters while she waits for her mom to arrive. Plus, it'd be nice to clear her head after all the studying she'd been doing for the past few weeks in preparation for her final exams. She had one left. It was for her English class but wouldn't be until next week. She was feeling pretty confident for that one and was glad it wouldn't require as much studying as her other classes. Caitlynn by far has never been a straight A student, although she has had her fair share, she mostly attains B's in her course work which will be plenty enough for her to either enroll in UNC Asheville or Coastal Carolina next fall. She hadn't quite made up her mind whether she wanted to stay in Yawnoc and attend CCU or to take the leap and head for the mountains. It has always been a dream of hers to live in the mountains where it snows and to operate her own Veterinarian clinic there one day. That isn't to say she hasn't felt a tug from the good ole town of Yawnoc either. As much as she loves the mountains, there's just something about her little town that has always had a special place in her heart.

Probably always will.

In a way that is just hard to explain, it's like she has a soul connection to this little town. Like something inside just knows this is where she is supposed to be. Besides, with the way things are with her health, it's probably best if she did stay put in Yawnoc. Her family is here. Her friends are here. Her life is here, and probably always will be.

As Caitlynn plays with these thoughts, she begins to scan the crowd for any sign of Phil from yesterday. Ned's Diner is just a few blocks ahead, and so far, there's no sign of Phil. The strangeness of their encounter and now his seeming disappearance is not lost on her. Is he okay? Did he get jumped last night and was left in the woods somewhere. She stands outside of Ned's for a moment and searches the streets, but Phil is nowhere to be seen. Caitlynn shakes her head and enters the diner. She sees the older lady and teenage boy behind the counter and the auburn-haired waitress making her rounds. Caitlynn takes the seat near the window where the three jeering men were yesterday. She keeps a check outside for Phil. After a moment, the waitress stops by and asks if she needed anything. Caitlynn tells her she's good for now and just waiting for someone. She checks her phone to see it's about twenty to noon. She reaches into her purse and pulls out the copy of Anthony Gerald's latest book. She had it marked on page twenty-three with a Kohl's receipt. She was using it until she could find her good bookmark. She just had it the other day when she finished reading her Colleen Hoover novel. Anyhow, until then, Kohl's receipt it is. Also tucked away inside her purse is a small notepad. It's filled with everything from sketches, half-finished poems, and her inner thoughts and philosophy. In a way, she figured it was a diary of sorts. It was something she had started as a pre-teen and had fiddled with it off and on through the years. Over the last few months though it's become a daily habit to add something to the little notebook. Lately, the daily entries have mostly been poems. She contributed the recent spark to her English course this semester as the professor had challenged the students to begin journaling daily to help manage their stress and inner dialogue.

About a month ago, Caitlynn had begun working on a poem she had titled *Our first step towards home*. A melody of words had come to her while showering late one night after a grueling study session. She had to rush out of the shower and thumb the words into her iPhone's note app. Since then, she had only added a few lines. The words were straight from her heart and were a little scary to pen down if she were honest. The theme of the poem was mostly centered around death and the afterlife. It was mostly an accumulation of her worries of dying young, which she had had since she first began journaling over a decade ago. Though she had all these great ambitions in life, somehow, she always felt she was running short of time. Like the hourglass had been switched to fast forward mode and the sand was rushing to empty.

Caitlynn pulls away from her book. She had made it to page twenty-eight but had hardly comprehended anything she'd read. Nothing against the book. Her mind was just too scattered at the moment. She adds her Kohl's receipt to the center crease and places the book on the table. She looks out the window. Still no sign of Phil.

As she busies herself with scanning the crowd of passing people, a phrase comes to her. A melody of words as she likes to call them. *Death is a journey we all must make alone. For it is but our first step towards home.* She lets the words marinate. They play on repeat above all the noise in the diner. She hears Alan Jackson singing a Christmas song from the jukebox in the corner of the room, and hears people talking, but it's this phrase that screams at the forefront of her mind. Everything else is like elevator music. There, but not only in the background.

Caitlynn whispers the words to herself, "Death is a journey we all must make alone. For it is but our first step towards home."

She reaches into her purse and retrieves her notepad. As she finishes jotting down the last line, she hears the bell chime above the door. She looks and finds her mother stepping inside.

"Over here, Mom."

Her mother follows her voice and smiles when she sees her. "Whew, let me tell you. Traffic on 501 is nuts out there. I'm glad I left when I did."

"It was slow for me too."

Her mom removes her coat and gloves and takes her seat. "Have you ordered yet?"

"No, I was waiting for you," Caitlynn says as she slides her novel and note-book back into her purse.

Her mom nods then looks around the diner for the waitress. She waves her over when she spots her.

The two place their orders and continue chit chatting while they wait. Before Caitlynn knows it, the topic of her parents' marriage comes up. Not that she didn't expect it, for it was her mother who wanted to meet for lunch. After yesterday's conversation, she knew this was likely going to be the subject of their discussion.

"I mean I'm sure you guys will be fine. You're just going through a rough patch, ya know."

Her mom sighs and looks out the window.

"Not everyone is as optimistic as you Caitlynn."

She wrinkles her brows and cranes her head, "Well, not everyone is as pessimistic as you, Mom."

She watches her mom bite the inside of her lip and turn to stare at her.

"Look, all I'm saying is maybe you should try focusing on all the things he does right instead of focusing on what he does wrong. Like, maybe try writing down everything you like and appreciate about Dad and have him do the same about you. I'm not saying for you to ignore each other's faults and mistakes, I'm just simply saying maybe you should shift your focus to each other's positive attributes for a change. You know, an attitude of gratitude sort of thing. At least, will you give it a try?"

Her mom breathes deeply and keeps her eyes on Caitlynn. Finally, as the waitress is bringing their food, her mother bobs her head and grins. At the same moment, Caitlynn's phone goes off. *Grand Strand Oncology* lights up her screen.

"Do you need to take that?" Her mom asks.

Caitlynn breaks her stare from the phone, clears her throat, and says, "No. It can wait. It's not important. Well, let's dig in, shall we?"

She feels her phone vibrate to indicate a voicemail. Her stomach twists into a knot and she has to force an appetite on herself. Her mom smiles with a cheekful of sandwich. Caitlynn returns the gesture. The thought of the voicemail and what the doctor had perhaps said on the other line takes center stage in her mind.

Caitlynn keeps her composure and manages to get through the lunch with her mom without her asking any probing questions. She would eventually tell them of what's going on, but not now. Now isn't the time.

†††

AFTER GETTING TO BED early that night but staying up late getting lost in her Anthony Gerald novel, Caitlynn eventually caught herself dozing off around one-thirty. She'd been so engrossed in the story that the sense of time had simply escaped her. The sleep she succumbed to was deep and all encompassing. She awoke the next morning to the tune of her alarm in the same position as when she had closed her eyes the night before. But just as she was swimming to the surface of consciousness, images of her dream painted the rooms of her mind. The memory of it swallowed her like a wave.

In the dream, she was walking along a crowded street. She could feel in her heart, she was searching for someone. She remembers feeling like a child lost from their mother. That empty, sinking feel of separation gnawed at her. She could feel herself becoming desperate as she pushed through the crowd. In the distance, she was able to make out the back of a man dressed in a long, white robe. Her heart leapt within her, and she quickened her pace. A gentle voice began calling to her.

Death is a journey we all must make alone.

For it is but our first step towards home.

The voice grew louder as she drew near. The sound of the crowd was muted. She could hear the footsteps of the man in the robe. Caitlynn came within a few yards of him and stopped. The crowd was frozen into place. She watched as the man began to turn and face her. As he did so, she recognized the white beard, white curly hair, and those deep, dark blue eyes.

It was Phil.

He smiled at her without showing teeth. She could hear his voice, but his lips didn't move. He repeated those words until she awoke.

Death is a journey we all must make alone.

For it is but our first step towards home.

After sitting at the edge of her bed and recalling the dream, Caitlynn crossed the room and took up her notebook sitting atop a bookshelf. She returned to the edge of her bed. After a moment had passed, she was able to add another three lines to her poem, building on the words from Phil and thinking back to the dream. She finished racking her brain and sat the notebook aside. Caitlynn got ready for work, but the whole time her mind was on the dream.

She made it to work around ten minutes till eight and settled in behind her monitor at the receptionist desk. An hour passes without any visitors, and Caitlynn and her co-worker, Jessica, were just talking of it being a slow morning when an older woman comes waddling up to the glass door. The commotion grabs Caitlynn and Jessica's attention. The old lady looks to be carrying a small Chihuahua and struggles opening the door. Caitlynn rushes from behind the desk and pushes open the door.

The old lady is in tears.

"Please. Please. You have to help him. You have to help my baby."

"Okay, ma'am. Okay. We're here to help. Take a breath for me, okay?" Caitlynn says holding the door open with her foot and looking closely at the dog. His face appears swollen and puffy.

"What happened ma'am?" Caitlynn asks as they both step inside.

"I'd let him out to use the bathroom and the next thing I know I hear him squealing. I rushed out to grab him and he's scrunching his face up like something bit him."

"Likely too cold to be bees or a snake," Caitlynn mumbles aloud as they make their way to the back room to see the vet.

Jessica follows behind them.

Caitlynn pets the dog in the lady's arm and asks, "What's his name, ma'am?"

"Elvis."

Caitlynn snickers, "Well aren't you a cool little dude."

"Oh, please help him. Please, you have to do something," the old lady says with tears running down her cheeks.

Caitlynn rubs her arm and says, "We will ma'am. Elvis will be just fine. Okay? Now, let's get you seated in this room right here and Jessica is going to grab our vet, okay?"

The old lady sniffles and follows the directions.

Caitlynn continues to soothe both the lady and dog.

After the vet checks things out, it appears Mr. Elvis had stumbled into a fire ant mound and taken a few dozen bites to the feet and snout. Luckily, it wasn't as bad as it all seemed. Other than swelling and some irritability, Mr. Elvis would be back to his old self within a day or two tops.

The old lady thanked Caitlynn with a good hug and the two were on their way.

It was just after twelve o'clock when the lady had left, so Caitlynn grabbed her purse and headed for the parking lot. She was to meet Alexandria at twelve thirty for lunch.

As she had witnessed the old lady's devotion and love to Mr. Elvis, a few lines of poetry had come to her. She made mental notes of the lines and was sure to jot them into her notepad when she reached her car. She had no intention of finishing the poem, if one could even call it that, but found that her mind didn't stop with the few lines she thought of at work. Before she even realized it, she was lost in a trancelike state and the pen flew with grace and speed. Within a matter of minutes, her melody of words as she liked to call it, was complete. She pulled back and stared at the pages for a moment. There were twenty-one lines in total. One for each year of her life she guesses. These aren't just words to her. They're from her heart. Her very soul. She feels her spirit connect to them like metal to a magnet. They're pieces of her.

Caitlynn lets out a deep breath and wipes a tear from her eye. She swallows hard and turns over the ignition. About a mile down the road, she gets a phone call. Probably Alexandria. It wasn't.

The name on the screen sends a hammer to her heart. Her pulse soars and she licks her lips. A knot forms in her gut. She almost doesn't answer it. It was just entering the fifth ring when she forced herself to pick up.

The doctor's voice was crisp and to the point. No sugar coating or false hope. He simply delivered the facts and nothing more. Caitlynn asked if he was sure. He said he was and with certainty. He apologized for the news but said at least she still had options. Whatever hope that was supposed to give.

Caitlynn sniffled and wiped her eyes with the sleeve of her shirt. As she approached an intersection, she asked the doctor a question. The doctor was in mid-sentence when Caitlynn caught glimpse of something white racing towards her. At that moment, everything entered into slow-motion. Her five senses kicked into high gear. She could feel her feet planted onto the floor of her car. Could feel the back of her legs resting in the seat. Felt the seat belt putting pressure on her shoulder and chest. She could feel the steering wheel digging into her hands as she squeezed with every ounce of strength she had until it felt like the wheel would bend as if made from rubber. She could still taste the wintergreen gum even though she had spit it out before she got into her car. She could smell the cinnamon air freshener hanging from her mirror. The sound of squealing brakes ripped through the air. Her vision turned to a bright white as images of her life flash before her as if on a projector screen. She heard a tremendous crash, followed by a roaring sound that made her think she was standing next to a jet airliner. The white projector screen of her life slowly faded away. Her senses did the same.

Before she knew it, she was drifting into nothingness. Like a dreamless sleep, Caitlynn was no more.

6

The sun had set, and a brisk breeze had settled over the town. The limbs swayed to send dead leaves spinning to the earth. Christmas music played over loud, outdoor speakers. People's breath steamed into the air. It was ten minutes to seven and a crowd was gravitating towards the ginormous Christmas Tree in the center of downtown Yawnoc. The Grindalls joined them and enjoyed their cups of hot cocoa.

"Will Santa be here?" asks Samuel as he walks between Eli and Emily while holding each of their hands.

"I don't think so honey. He's probably busy building toys at the North Pole," says Emily.

"I wish he was here so I could ask him if he's found me a puppy yet."

Eli looks down at him and says, "Son, me and Santa had a discussion, and you'll need to ask for something else this year, okay?"

Eli feels Samuel's shoulders sag.

"But I want a puppy, Dad. What's so wrong with me having a puppy? I'll take care of it."

"I know you will, Son. But not this year, okay? Maybe once you're older."

Eli feels Emily give him a glare.

Samuel sighs then points ahead and yells, "Oh my gosh, look at how big those candy canes are. Are they for real?"

Eli chuckles, "It looks that way. You want one?"

"Heck yeah, I want one."

Emily joins Eli in his chuckles.

Samuel gets his candy cane and the Grindalls make their way over to the tree where carolers sing to their heart's desire. When they finished singing, a round bellied man with glasses, khakis, and a red dress shirt stepped to the center and spoke into a mic. He introduced himself as the city manager and began by thanking everyone for attending before telling a bit of back story for the star on the top of the tree. He talked about the wise men in the Bible and made a little joke about how they all must have been firemen because scripture says they came from *a far*. The man adds to his already southern accent for effect on the play of words. The crowd erupts into laughter.

The city manager finishes by saying, "May this light serve as reminder that the Light of the World has come and lived among us. He forsook his life in paradise so we could all have a chance of eternity in heaven with Him one day. May we always remember his sacrifice and that no matter how dark this ole world gets, His light shines on for all to see."

The crowd applauds.

The city manager dips his head and says, "Alright. Thank you. Thank you. Alright now, on the count of three we'll get this baby lit. Okay, one . . . two."

The crowd says it with him.

Eli looks down at Samuel and Samuel looks up at him with a big, toothy grin. Together they say, *three.*

The star flashes bright to pierce the night.

Emily draws near to him and wraps her arm around Eli's waist. He hugs her back. Samuel comes around to the left of him and Eli drapes his hand over Samuel's shoulder.

"Thank you for doing this," Emily says.

Eli looks at her and sees tears filling her eyes.

Eli kisses the top of her head and says, "Honey, you don't have to thank me."

She nods and wipes her nose.

Eli squeezes her and adds, "I'm glad we did this. We needed it, didn't we?"

"Yes, we did. We should do stuff like this more often."

Eli agreed, then said a silently prayer that God would help him with things at work so he could be the husband and father he should be. He feels a knot grow in his throat and now his own eyes become moist.

The Grindalls spend another hour at the event before calling it a night. On the way home, Eli tells Emily he'll drop them off at home because he needs to spend a few hours at the office to finish up on some things. Emily gives her protest, but Eli wins her over by promising he's almost finished and real soon he could be getting back to a normal work schedule. Emily is reluctant to give in, but with enough promising and smiles, Eli succeeds.

It was close to nine when he reached the office. He settles in behind his desk and boots up his monitor. He crosses the room and digs around a file cabinet. Eli finds what he needs and returns to his desk with the files from his secretary and a record of the balance sheets from last quarter.

An hour later he gets a text from his business partner. It read, *CALL ME ASAP!! WE NEED TO TALK! TONIGHT!*

"What they heck?" Eli says while staring at the words.

He places the call. Grant answers on the second ring.

"Eli."

"Grant, what's up?"

"Listen, I'll keep this short and sweet. I'm out. I'm done. I can't go through another lawsuit with you. It's not worth it. I'm lucky to still have my family from the last one."

"Whoa. Whoa. Whoa. Grant, hold up a second. What's going on?"

"I'm done, Eli. It's over. I know we've been through thick and thin through the years, but this is just too much, man."

"Grant, don't do me like this."

Grant was quiet for a minute before adding, "You've done it to yourself, Eli."

Eli cursed and slammed his fist onto the desk. He gritted his teeth and said, "You're a coward, you know that? You're a coward."

"Makes no difference what you think about me, Eli. I honestly couldn't care less. You know, I've seen this coming for a while now. I should've already walked away. You're lucky I didn't."

"I thought you were a friend, Grant."

Grant snorted and said, "I thought you were too, Eli. I thought you were too."

The line goes quiet.

"I need my share, Eli. I need my twenty-five percent."

"You know I can't do that. Not right now. I'm going to be doing good to pay the attorney fees to get things started."

"Well, I guess you better be figuring something out then."

Eli cursed him.

"You're going to get me my share or you'll have more to worry about than paying attorney fees."

Eli started to protest, but he heard the line drop.

He shoved back from the desk to send the chair toppling over onto the floor. Eli swiped his desk free of its clutter and screamed at the ceiling. If someone was walking nearby outside, they may be inclined to believe a murder was taking place.

Eli's breath escaped faster than he could take it in. Sweat beads trickled down his forehead. He could feel his heart struggling to keep a rhythm. His head began to spin. A dark shadow appeared in the corner of his eye. Eli felt a douse of gooseflesh spread over him. He turned for a better look. Nothing was there. A footstep emitted from the other side of the room. Eli spun around and let out a yelp when a tall man in a dark rob filled his vision. Eli felt his entire body begin to tremble. The man's face was hidden deep within the hood. As Eli was about to confront the man, a numbing, tingling sensation fired up his arm and pierced his heart. The pain was so crippling, it caused him to double over. His breath had now become a gasp and before he knew it, Eli was collapsing onto the floor. The carpet burned his cheek when he landed with a thud and slid to a halt. His heart felt like it had a dagger sticking in it. His pulse thumped hard in the veins along his neck. Eli kept blinking his eyes as a strong sense of sleepiness had settled over him. He could see the man in the dark robe still standing there and glaring down at him while not saying a word. Eli's cell phone lay on the floor in front of him. His vision blurred. Eli stretched forth his hand.

The phone was just out of reach.

Eli began to slip out of this world and into another.

The room was turning dark.

He stretched again for the phone. He felt it kiss his fingertips. He shifted closer. Out of his peripheral, he watched the tall man move towards him.

His heart screamed in agony. His breath stuck in his throat. He felt himself drift again. He bit down on his bottom lip and squeezed hard enough to draw blood. Anything to keep himself awake.

He stretched again, took hold of the phone, and dialed those three lifesaving numbers. A voice answered. Eli couldn't make out the words, but started mumbling before all went dark for a final time.

7

Caitlynn awoke to something cool and damp lapping against her face. She could hear a gentle breeze ruffling some leaves nearby. She could feel she was lying on her back on a lush patch of grass. Birds sang and chirped overhead. A warm ray of sunlight embraced her. Caitlynn rose and began opening her eyes. A vast meadow full of striking colors on either side of a crystal-clear river filled her sight. The licks to the face continued. She turned to find her favorite dog from childhood, Girl-Girl, who was a black and brown border collie, sitting next to her.

"Oh my gosh, Girl-Girl. What are you doing here?"

Caitlynn wrapped her arms around the dog's neck and gave her a good squeeze. Girl-Girl returned the love with more licks to the face.

As the initial excitement of seeing Girl-Girl began to wane, logic settled over her. Girl-Girl had been dead for six years now. Caitlynn was in the room with her when the vet had to put her down. That experience was a big reason why Caitlynn decided she wanted to be a vet in the first place. Caitlynn gulped as the realization settled over her.

"I've missed you so much. You have no idea," Caitlynn says to her as the dog sits there with a smiling pant.

Caitlynn stands to her feet and dusts off her clothes. She puts a hand up to shield the radiant sun. Everything is so surreal. The colors all have a unique sparkle and shine to them. The meadow is filled with lavender and lilies. Huge, snow capped mountains stand guard as far as the eye can see. A herd of deer roams near the river. A pack of wolves wander next to them. They walk together without strife or chaos. On the other side of the river are an abundance of large trees with bright red fruits the size of watermelons hanging from white blooms.

The beauty and perfection of all that she sees is overwhelming. All she can do is stand in awe as she tries to take everything in.

"I felt the same way when I first arrived." A gentle voice sounded from behind her.

Caitlynn spun around to find an angelic lady in a white gown standing with her shoulder against the tree Caitlynn had awoken beneath. The lady had a radiant smile, striking ocean-colored eyes, and long, dark hair. She appeared to be around middle-aged, but her beauty was unlike anything Caitlynn had seen. She just had such a grace and pureness to her that it was hard to describe.

"Is. Is. Is this heav . . ." Caitlynn didn't finish.

The lady smiled and nodded before striding closer to her.

"Yes, this is heaven," the lady said as she waved her hand about the land.

"My goodness. It's beautiful."

"It is indeed. Our creator has quite the imagination."

The lady looks at Caitlynn and Caitlynn looks at her.

They began to laugh heartedly before embracing in a hug. They share joyous laughter for a long moment while swaying side to side. Finally, a thought occurs to Caitlynn, and she pulls back from the lady.

"What about my family?" she asks as she is suddenly taken with a deep longing for them.

The lady gives a graceful smile and squeezes both of Caitlynn's elbows as she looks her in the eye and says, "They will join you here one day too, but until then, you will be tasked with watching over them. The Creator will give you opportunity to visit them from time to time and to remind them of what awaits." The lady ended with once again, extending her hand about the land.

"I already miss them so much. It hurts deep in my soul. I thought there was no pain in heaven?"

The lady smiles again and rubs Caitlynn's back while saying, "That is not pain, my child, that is love."

Caitlynn swallows hard and looks down at Girl-Girl who sits there smiling up at her. Caitlynn nods her head in agreement with the lady's profound statement.

"Now, I need you to listen up for a second. I am to deliver an important message directly from the great Creator himself."

Caitlynn looks at her and nods.

"You have been given an assignment. It is urgent and important. One that will need your decision immediately. Okay?"

"Of course," Caitlynn says while wrinkling her brows.

"The assignment will depend on this decision."

"Okay."

"Now. You have two choices. You can go back to be with your family. Live well into your nineties and see that all of your hopes and dreams are fulfilled. Or you can stay here and wait for your family's arrival. Now, if you decide to stay here, your choice will be giving life and a second chance to someone who can at times, be a cruel man. Your assignment will then be to guard this man and help him change his perspective. If you do go back, this man will die. What will your decision be?"

Caitlynn swallowed the knot in her chest and turned to look out over the vast beauty before them. She took a moment to soak it all in. Then she closed her eyes, breathed deep, and thought about her family. The pain of missing them weighed heavy on her heart. She thought about this man the lady spoke of. Did he deserve this second chance? Probably not, but then again, who really does?

Caitlynn turned back to the lady and asked, "What is his name?"

"Eli. Eli Grindall."

"So, if I did this, I would basically be sacrificing my life to give this man a second chance?"

The lady nodded.

Caitlynn ran her hands through her hair and rested them on the back of her neck. She shut her eyes and pondered the scenario. After a long moment, Caitlynn raised her vision to the meadow.

She turned to the lady and asked, "And I can check on my family and offer support through . . . through everything?"

"Yes. You will be able to watch over them and offer comfort until their arrival. It will be difficult for them, but your presence will get them through it."

"Will my parents stay together?"

"That I can not promise. Things like this are difficult for everyone, but I promise you can be there to help them through it. You have my word."

Caitlynn sighed and looked over the meadow. A flock of bright colored birds flew down below in the meadow. Caitlynn looked at Girl-Girl and patted her head.

"What will it be, my child?"

Caitlynn drew a long breath and looked at the woman, "I will give this man a second chance. God knows we could all use one."

The lady smiles and says, "I will let the Creator know."

8

li could hear a muffled voice in the distance.

It was garbled like it came from under water. His body felt weightless, like there was no gravity. He seemed to be caught between that dark space of reality and dream. Something beeped. He could hear footsteps.

"Hey . . . time to wake up," the voice said as someone nudged his leg.

Eli groaned and began opening his eyes. His head throbbed with a killer hangover. Except he doesn't remember drinking the night before. In fact, he can't even recall the last time he'd drank enough to induce a hangover like this. The top of his head felt like it could split open any second, so Eli kept a hand there just in case. He massaged his head and blinked at the sight before him. He was in a hospital room. Lying in the bed was himself. Eli was looking at himself. His heart leapt within him as a cold, ghostly finger caressed the back of his neck. His blood turned to ice water straight from the Artic Circle. He rubbed his arms and felt the gooseflesh festering across his skin. Seated next to the hospital bed was his wife, Emily. She gripped his hand, gently rubbing it, and had her head buried in the bed sheets next to him. A nurse walked in and checked the dozen or so IV drips.

Eli begins to stand from the recliner in the corner but feels a heavy hand press down on his shoulder. Eli looks up to see the homeless man from the street staring back at him. Those blue eyes glare deep into his soul. Eli swallowed and sat back down. He watched the man step in front of him while keeping his eyes focused on the Eli in the hospital bed.

Eli tried to speak, but his lips trembled so much he only stuttered.

The man turned around and looked at him.

"Who-who-wh—"

The man patted down the air with both hands and said, "Relax. Okay?"

"What happened? Am I? Am I . . ." Eli trailed off as he just couldn't bring himself to ask the question.

The man shook his head, "Not quite."

"Who? Who are you?"

"Names Phil. Who I am is not what's important though."

Eli watches Phil turns his attention back to the Eli in bed with all the tubes sticking out of him.

"What happened?"

"You had a massive heart attack, my friend. You're lucky to still be breathing. If they hadn't have got to you when they did, you'd for sure be a goner."

"Why am I still hanging on? I mean why are you here?"

"Because I've been sent by the Creator. You've been given a second chance."

"What? Why me?"

Phil smirks, "Hmph. Why any of us?" He looks back at him and adds, "Listen up. Here's the deal. You're going to pull through this, but you will be given two choices. Okay?"

Eli feels his Adam's Apple bob as he nods his head.

"Good. Now come with me. I need to show you something."

Eli watches Phil turn and head for the door. His long, tattered trench coat drags the floor. Eli stands from the recliner and follows him. Phil waits on the other side of the door. Eli turns and looks at his wife one last time. Tears well in his eyes and he says, "I'm sorry, babe. Be strong."

She raises her head and glances about the room as if she may have heard him. He watches her wipe her cheeks and sniffle. Phil pats his shoulder. Eli sighs and turns around. Phil stands in the hallway.

The moment Eli stepped through the door, his entire body was jerked forward as if sucked by a vacuum cleaner. The wind rushed at him and wrinkled his face. His breath was caught in his lungs. It felt like he was driving down the interstate with his head hanging out the window. At once, the wind ceased, and Eli stumbled forward into the front yard of his home. Dead leaves covered the tall grass and some of them skittered across the sidewalk when the wind blew. Phil waddled along in front of him. Eli was taken back by the condition of the home. Green, black mildew had spread across the white siding and a few of the pieces were hanging loose to reveal the Tyvek beneath it. The wood on the front porch was worn and dilapidated. Eli looked over to the driveway and found an old pick-up truck sitting on blocks. A pontoon boat sat on its trailer in the grass next to the driveway. The cover of the motor was missing, and leaves lay scattered across the carpet. About that time, Eli hears a loud, clunky engine roaring down the street.

"Please God, no."

A black SUV pulls into the driveway behind the old truck sitting on blocks. Eli leans down and peers through the front windshield. Emily sits in the passenger seat, and some bearded man is behind the wheel.

Eli turns and looks at Phil who stands next to the front door with his hands in his coat pockets. Phil tightens his lips and shrugs.

Eli hears the car doors slam as voices fill the air. He turns around to find Emily and this mystery man striding along the sidewalk. Emily had gained at least forty pounds and was only a ghost of her former self. Her complexion was pale, and her eyes carried black bags beneath them. The man had a big beer belly, a scruffy beard, and sad eyes. Emily and the man were arguing about something, but that wasn't what held Eli's attention. It was the teenage boy getting out from the back seat of the car. Eli blinked and rubbed his eyes. He felt his jaw drop and he spun to look back at Phil. Phil sucked on his teeth and looked down at his feet. Eli looked back at the teenager.

"There's no way."

Samuel was dressed in all black and had black fingernails, black eye liner, and long black hair. If he was competing in a Halloween goth costume contest, he'd no doubt walk away with the grand prize. Eli watched as Samuel walked past him with his eyes fixed to his phone and wireless earbuds stuck in his ears.

"Son, what have you done?" Eli says, but no one notices. Eli watches as the three of them enter the home.

Phil stands to the side with his hands behind his back.

Eli marches up to him and grabs his coat collar. He shoves Phil against the side of the home.

"What happened? Why are you showing me this?" Tears fill his eyes, and his words are choked off at the end. Eli feels his strength leave him and he releases Phil. Eli crumbles to the ground and buries his face into his hand.

"This is what will happen if you continue to live the way you've been living. Your business will go bankrupt, you and Emily will divorce, she'll remarry a charming, narcissistic creep who'll come and sweep her off her feet, only to leave her and Samuel trapped inside their own home. The one that will be paid for from your alimony, mind you. You'll basically be paying to have the creep mistreat and take advantage of your family."

"God, no. Please. Please. Don't let that happen. Please, I'll do anything."

Phil waddles over to him and picks him up by his armpits. He stands to his feet and Phil waves a hand about the front yard. A projector screen flashes before them. A movie of Eli's life begins to play. Phil commentates as the film rolls.

"You yourself will be so burdened by all the stress and bills that'll you'll be forced to work two jobs just to stay afloat. You'll eventually have a mental breakdown. Shortly afterwards you'll resort to life on the streets."

A clip of Eli dressed in beggar's clothes and rattling a paper cup flashes on the screen. People pass by and sneer at him. Eli remembers back to his first encounter with Phil on the street. He'd do anything to go back and treat the man differently.

"You'll become a bitter man and will die a lonely death."

The scene cuts to a grave side funeral. Emily and Samuel stand there next to the beer bellied man. Both Emily and Samuel have black eyes and bruised cheeks.

By now, Eli is sobbing and hanging onto Phil's coat.

"Please. Please, don't let this happen. I'm begging you."

"It's not my decision to make, Eli. I'm simply the messenger. Only you can decide what happens. If you continue to live the way you've been living, that there is your outcome."

"Turn it off. Please, I don't want to see anymore."

"Hold up, I have one last thing to show you. On the other hand, if you lean into the change the Creator wants to make in your life, this could be your outcome."

The screen flashes to a beautiful back yard filled with children both young and in their teens, playing and running about with laughter pouring out from them. An elderly couple sit in a swing on the porch. The lady has her head lying upon the old man's shoulder. The family is filled with so much love, Eli can feel it in his bones. He smiles and crosses his arms while resting his chin in one hand. The children's laughter penetrates the air. The tall oak trees sway with the breeze and creak with the movement.

Phil lets Eli soak it all in for a long moment before finally waving his hand through the air. The screen disappears.

Eli sniffles and wipes his eyes with the sleeve of his shirt. "Please, just take me back to my family. You've made your point, okay?"

Phil gives a gentle grin and dips his head.

Eli's world turns black.

9

Caitlynn's first assignment is to visit her family. With the angelic lady as her guide, they appear in the living room of Caitlynn's parent's home. The room is crowded with the immediate family. She finds her parents seated on the couch with her grandfather next to her mother and her aunt next to her father. A dry eye was nowhere to be found as she watched them all take turns passing Kleenex's. An emptiness she couldn't explain filled her being and she longed for their embrace.

Caitlynn looked at the lady still dressed in her long, white gown. The lady smiled and nodded.

Caitlynn strode over to her mother and squatted down to be eye level with her. She interlocked her hands behind her mother's neck and leaned her forehead against her mother's.

"I love you so much, Mom. Sshh. Sshh. Please, don't cry. I'm okay. I promise," Caitlynn managed to say through her tears.

Her mother sniffles and dabs her eyes. Caitlynn hugs her. She holds her like this for a good minute before letting go. Her mother swallows hard and looks at the people in the room.

"She's here. I can feel her."

Caitlynn's grandpa pats her leg and says, "She'll always be here, Honey. Always."

Caitlynn stood and walked over to her dad. She hugged him too and offered soothing words.

"Oh Dad, don't cry. It's going to be alright. I promise."

She squeezed his neck then kissed his forehead.

"Caitlynn," she heard the lady say.

She looked at her. The lady gave a tilt of her head and said, "C'mere. I need to tell you something."

Caitlynn drew near and turned to look at her family once more.

The lady placed her hands on Caitlynn's shoulders and pulled her attention before saying, "Tonight, you will visit your mother in a dream. It will be brief, but it is important that you tell her not to give up. She must stay strong."

Caitlynn swallows the knot in her throat and nods.

"Will they stay together? This won't separate them, will it?"

"That isn't for me to say, my child. Only time will tell."

Caitlynn rubs the back of her neck and asks, "How often can I visit them?"

"As often as you like per the Creator's permission."

Caitlynn looks back at her family.

"There are other ways you can show your presence, you know."

"Yeah, like what?"

"While visitations and dreams are important, the use of red Cardinals and yellow butterflies are another way to show your presence. Some like to leave behind pennies for their loved ones to find. There are other ways, but these are the most common."

"How does that work?"

"Well, you will be notified by myself when your family is in need of encouragement, and you can then choose how you want to manifest."

A moment passes between them as Caitlynn considers her words. "Maybe I should've chosen to stay with them. I mean, is this guy I'm given a second chance to really worth it?"

"Hmph. Everyone is worth it, my child. Everyone."

Caitlynn looks back at the lady and says, "I didn't mean it that way. I was meaning—"

"I know what you meant," she says as she pats Caitlynn's arm.

"I just hate seeing my family like this. I wish I could physically hug them and talk to them."

"You will, my child. You will."

"What? When?"

"That's what the dreams are for."

"When will that happen?"

"Tonight."

10

His mind swam with a million thoughts at once as it felt like it'd been tossed into an angry, chaotic sea. A constant beeping filled the air as a dull ache lingered in his chest. The taste of bile was present on his tongue. A sharp aroma of disinfectant stung his nostrils. Despite his confused state, Eli knew he was in a hospital room even before he opened his eyes. When he did, the sound of Emily's gasp brought a smile to his face. She threw her arms around him and began to weep. Eli winced as she laid on top of him. Emily heard his discomfort and pulled back while wiping her eyes.

"Oh honey. Oh honey," was all she could say as she squeezed his hand.

Eli smiled and squeezed back. She leaned in and gave him a long kiss. When she finished, Eli began to scan the room for Phil. To his relief, it was only he and Emily.

"Oh God, it's so good to have you back. I thought I lost you, Eli," Emily got choked up and continued with, "For God's sake, I thought I lost you."

Emily placed a hand on his head and cried.

Eli squeezed her other hand and cleared his throat. His lips were dry and cracked. "I'm here, sweetie. I'm here."

Emily sniffled and stepped away with a hand to her forehead. "I need to call the doctor. They need to get in here." She said before coming to him and pressing a red button near his bed.

Moments later, two nurses and a doctor entered the room.

"Why hello, Mr. Grindall. It's good to have you with us. I'm Doctor Montgomery. How are you feeling? Any pain or nausea?"

Eli adjusted in the bed and swallowed with a wince before saying, "I feel like I've been run over by a transferred truck then left in the desert to die."

They all share a laugh at that.

Doctor Montgomery says something to one of the nurses who then walks over to assess an IV bag.

The lady doctor, who is petite, blonde and perhaps middle aged, looks at Eli and says, "We'll up your pain meds to help relax you and keep you calm. You're a lucky man, Mr. Grindall. Most people who suffer such a cardiac event as severe as the one you have, do not live to see another day. You may want to thank your lucky stars because I think someone up there has given you a second chance."

Eli felt hot tears form as his lips began to tremble. A warm sensation came over him. He swallows hard and looks at his chest. A thick red line snake its way down to his naval. Thick black staples keep the seam together.

"My goodness, you about cut me in two."

The doctor raises her brows and tilts her head, "Just be thankful we had a reason to leave you with that scar. If your donor hadn't of had been so generous, you'd have died that night."

"So, I have someone else's heart in here?" Eli asks while angling his chin to his chest.

"That's right. You two were a perfect match and were only a few towns from each other. The other two matches we found were across the country and wouldn't have made it here in time."

Eli looks at the doctor and blinks away some tears then looks back at his chest and says, "There's someone else's heart in there."

"That's right, Mr. Grindall."

He sniffles and asks, "Who were they?"

Doctor Montgomery shifts her position and folds her hands in front of her. She draws a deep breath and looks at Eli and Emily. "Her name was Caitlynn Richards. She was twenty-one years old and of the same blood type as yourself. I can't give out much more information than that I'm afraid, but we can provide you with her family's contact should you later decide to speak with them."

Eli wipes his eyes free of tears and says with a cracked voice, "That would be great."

The nurse that was tending to the IV bag comes over and replaces the IV in his wrist. Once she's finished, Eli looks at Doctor Montgomery and asks, "What happened to Caitlynn? I mean she was healthy, right?"

The doctor drops her head and looks at the floor for a second. She shakes her head and looks back to him, "It was a car wreck. A teenager from the high school. He was likely texting if I had to guess. He ran straight through an intersection going fifty-five. As terrible as it was, luckily, Ms. Richards passed upon impact. It was a quick and painless death, I'm most certain."

"That poor child," Emily manages.

A moment passes between them. The nurses finish their work and leave the room.

Doctor Montgomery says, "You have a long recovery ahead of you Mr. Grindall, but with enough patience and perseverance, I'm confident you will come out stronger on the other side. You've been given a second chance at life, so I want you to always remember that." She finishes with tightening her lips and angling her chin at him.

Eli swallows hard and nods.

"It's good to see you awake Mr. Grindall. You're a walking miracle. Now, if you'll excuse me."

"Thank you, Doctor. I'm beyond grateful."

Montgomery dips her head and exits the room.

†††

Friday
December 22ⁿᵈ

ELI, EMILY, AND SAMUEL are seated around the kitchen table and enjoying a homemade breakfast of pancakes, eggs, and sausage that Emily had prepared. Eli lets out a deep breath and grimaces.

"You okay, Honey?" Emily asks after taking a sip of orange juice.

Eli gives her a reassuring nod.

Sam Cooke's *Bring it on home* lingers from the living room as Emily often changes the channel to one of the old music stations when she's cooking. The song takes him back to when they were younger and first falling in love. He recalls their dating days before thinking of the wedding. He thinks of the song he'd picked. It was Randy Travis' *Forever and ever, amen.* Eli smiles at the thought. It seems like just yesterday he was asking Emily out for dinner and a movie. Eli reaches out and squeezes Emily's hand as Sam Cooke reaches mid chorus.

"We used to dance to this, remember?"

Emily cranes her head and listens for a second. A smile stretches her lips and causes her cheeks to scrunch up against the bottom of her eyes. They still had that sparkle of emerald that'd stopped Eli in his tracks all those years ago. Emily nods her head and says, "We did, didn't we? Back when I was your girl as you always said."

Eli grins and says, "I love you, Sweetie. You'll always be my girl."

Emily blushes then leans in and kisses him.

Samuel covers his eyes and says, "Yuck. C'mon guys. Seriously? At the table?"

Eli and Emily shared a chuckle. The jarring is painful to Eli's chest. He winces and gives out a slight grunt.

"Sorry Kiddo," Eli says before taking up his cup of coffee. For as long as he could remember he had drunk his coffee black, but for some reason this morning he had the urge to mix it up a bit by adding a sizeable helping of cream along with two pink packs of sugar. The first sip was like heaven. He shut his eyes and soaked in the flavor.

As Sam Cooke's song ended and Rod Stewart's *You're in my heart* began, Eli found himself looking out the window into the front yard. A plethora of sparrows, finches, and black snowbirds littered all the little trees. A red cardinal stood out among all the others as Eli found himself entranced with its beauty. In that moment, a string of melodic words floated across his mind. The words were intriguing and potent. Profound. As he narrowed his gaze upon the cardinal, more words flowed to him. He felt like a conduit channeling an immense power he did not understand. He heard Emily's voice above Rod Stewart's. Her hand fell on his and brought him back. Eli cleared his throat and refocused his attention.

"You okay?" She asked.

Warm tears had stung his eyes and he felt one leak onto his lips. He licked it and brought a hand up to wipe the tears away. Eli tried to suppress the emotion building within as his mind repeated the words that'd come to him, but his resolve had left him. Gently, Eli began to weep. He crossed his arms and buried his face in his hands. His shoulders hitched and snot began to flow.

Emily stood from her chair and walked over to him. She hugged him from behind and planted her cheek against his.

Eli clung to her, and despite the dull ache in his chest, he continued to weep. After a good moment, Eli settled down and said through a choked voice, "I love you both so, so much. I'm sorry . . ." he struggled to finish his thoughts.

Emily stroked his hair and said, "Sshh. Sshh. Settle down now. You don't have to apologize."

Eli opened his eyes and pulled back. After wiping his tears, he looked out the window again to find the cardinal sitting along the window seal looking in on them. Eli blinked and the bird was gone.

His mind was then filled with the image of Phil from the streets. A sadness settled over him as he thought about all the homeless people who'd be missing out on family meals this Christmas. They were people too and were someone's parent, grandparent, aunt, uncle, brother, sister, you name it. They were people too. An urgency to do something filled his being. Then his mind lingered onto the subject of animal shelters and all the precious animals in need of a good home. He thought about Samuel's request to Santa for a puppy this year. Eli cursed himself for being such a hardnose. He looked at Samuel who was busy twiddling his thumbs and trying not to look at the mess his dad had suddenly become.

Eli looked at Emily and said, "I want to make a trip into town. There's something I want to do."

Emily wrinkled her brow at him.

"Trust me. I'm fine. Okay?"

"I just don't want you over doing it."

"I'm fine. It won't take just a minute."

Emily craned her head at him, "What are you wanting to do?"

"I'll tell you when we get in the car. It's a kind of a surprise."

Samuel looked up and studied him for a moment. Emily did the same.

Eli smiled.

†††

CAITLYNN FINDS HERSELF standing with the angelic lady again. Dogs bark and whine all around them. Caitlynn looks up to find the Grindalls coming down the long hallway as they're guided by a shelter worker. Caitlynn watches Samuel break from the group and rush to the cage where a handful of Husky puppies play. The boy squats down and talks to them.

Caitlynn turns and look at the lady, "Is he really going to let him have one?"

The lady gives a sheepish grin.

Caitlynn turns and watches Eli slowly shuffle his way over. Emily clings to his arm as if he'd fall over without her support.

"Oh. They're so cute," Samuel says as he sticks his fingers through the fence and lets the puppies take turns licking and chewing on them.

Caitlynn watches the boy's face sparkle with joy as he laughs and giggles. Eli's face on the other hand seems drained of its color. She sees his eyes are glued to the puppies.

"What's wrong with him? He looks like he's seen a ghost," Caitlynn says.

"It's a long story, but he had a husky once when he was a boy. Had a bad experience. I think he's recalling the memory, that's all," the lady answers.

Samuel ends up sitting on the ground next to the pin before looking up at Eli and saying, "Can I really have one, Dad?"

Eli blinks and clears his throat, "Let's get two while we're at it. That way they'll have a friend."

Samuel's eyes grow wide, and he drops his jaw in amazement. The boy stands and rushes over to wrap his arms around his father.

"Thank you. Thank you. Thank you."

"You're welcome, Son. Merry Christmas. Easy now."

Caitlynn watches Eli pat his son on the back before wiping a tear from his eye.

She smiles and looks to the lady, "This really is a new beginning for them, isn't it?"

The lady dips her head and says, "Yes, it is. It is indeed."

"Will it last?"

The lady cranes her head and says, "Only time will tell, my child. But always remember, bad people can change and even a bad man can do a good thing."

"I like that."

The lady smiles and says, "Me too."

As Caitlynn watched the Grindalls, a deep sleep settled over her and the scene before her began to fade like the remnants of a dream.

HAVING JUST LEFT THE shelter, the Grindalls begin the drive home. Emily drives so as to let Eli relax. Samuel is in heaven in the back seat with the two puppies.

Eli and Emily bask in his laughter.

"I haven't heard him this happy in a long time," Emily says as she glances in the rearview mirror.

Eli grins and turns to look back at him. "Me neither. And God is it good to hear."

Eli relaxes back into the seat and looks out the window to take in the scenery. The street is lined with red and green lights everywhere he looks. An orchestra plays *O Come All Ye Faithful* over the radio. Out of the corner of his eye he sees Emily's hand reach over to crank up the heat.

"You know, I've been thinking a lot about the business here recently," Eli says. He feels Emily look over at him.

"Yeah, I know."

"Not like that. I mean, I've been thinking of our future. I think we need to sell it."

"What? You've spent your entire life building this company."

"I know, but . . . it's time."

Emily gives it some thought then asks, "What about with the lawsuit and everything? How could you sell it with all that's going on?"

"Well, to the right investors, that's child's play."

"And by *right investors* you mean Bill in California?"

"He's definitely one I had in mind. He's been begging me for an entry for years. He has the experience and capital to turn things around. He could settle out of court with those goons at Bloomington and have things up and running in no time. I have some other people I think may be interested if he isn't."

Emily sighs, "I don't know Eli. I mean what will you do if you get rid of the company? We have to have a way to survive."

"I know. I thought that with the proceeds from the sale we could start that bed and breakfast business you've always dreamed about."

Emily cut her eyes at him, "Stop it. I know you're not serious about this."

"Does it look like I'm joking? Think about it. It'd be perfect. We'd finally have the time and capital to do it. We could run it together as a family business. You and me. And it'd be something we can leave behind for Samuel and his kids."

Emily brushes a strand of her dark hair away and looks in the rearview mirror again.

Eli reaches over and squeezes her hand, "Em, look at me. I really want to do this. For us. For our family. I don't want to go back to what I was doing. I'm done with that life. I want to do something we can build together. I'm tired of missing out and wasting time. I want to—"

Before he could finish, Emily cut in, "Then's let do it."

"For real?"

"Of course."

Eli squeezes her leg and leans over to kiss her cheek.

"I love you, Em. You're my girl. Always will be."

Eli pulls back, winces, and leans into the seat. He looks out the window in time to catch a glimpse of the soup kitchen. A line of about forty people spans from the doors to the sidewalk.

"Hold up. Stop. Turn in here."

"Do what?" Emily says.

"Put your turn signal on. Pull in here for a second."

Emily does as she's told. As she turns in and begins looking for a parking spot, Eli sees an elderly lady with a hair net and apron shutting the door to her older SUV.

"Stop right here," Eli says as he begins rolling down the window.

"What are you doing?" Emily asks.

"Excuse me. Excuse me, ma'am."

The lady turns around. She leans on a cane for support.

"How would one go about volunteering here?"

The old lady smiles, "Well, that's pretty simple. Just show up. We'll find a way to put you to work."

Eli chuckles and looks at the line of people waiting for a meal. "I bet y'all stay pretty busy this time of year, don't you?"

"Yes sir, we sure do. We could certainly use a hand. Especially this Sunday."

"Is that right?"

"Yes sir. We having a Christmas meal. Expecting a hundred people or more."

"Goodness. That many?"

"Yes sir. You'd be surprised how many don't have means for a good Christmas meal. The number seems to grow each year."

"Hmph. Tell you what . . ." Eli looks at Emily and Samuel then back to the old lady, "Count us in. What time does it start?"

"Be here at ten. Just c'mon on inside and we'll find something for you to do."

"Deal. I'm Eli by the way. What was your name, ma'am?"

"Nice to meet you, Eli. I'm Cecillia. Some folks call me Grandma Cilla. Makes no difference to me. I's answer to both."

They share a laugh before Eli says, "Nice to meet you too, Cecillia. We'll plan to see you Sunday."

†††

LATER THAT NIGHT as Emily is preparing for bed, Eli finds himself reading a Ted Dekker novel. Reading is something he's done a lot of over the recent weeks. He loved to read growing up but drifted from it after he got into college and the business took over his life. After the second day at home, he had a nag to be engrossed in a story again. It gnawed at him until finally, he asked Emily if she'd swing by the local bookstore in Yawnoc to pick up a few thriller or mystery books for him. He had read some of Dekker when his books first became popular, and remembered he really enjoyed them. He also remembered liking James Lee Burke, Cormac McCarthy, and Stephen King among others. These were the names he told Emily to look for during her search.

She made it back with about a dozen novels by these four authors. Which should be plenty to get him through his downtime.

Eli hears Emily turn off the sink faucet and flick the light switch to the bathroom. She crosses to the side of the bed and asks as she pulls the covers back to her side, "You're really enjoying those books, aren't you?"

"Huh?" Eli said peering down at her with his reading glasses at the end of his nose.

Emily chuckles.

"Sorry," Eli grins and secures his place with a bookmark. He sits the book on the nightstand and removes his glasses. He pinches his tear ducts and says, "I forgot how much I enjoyed reading."

"Well, that's good. Hey, I noticed when I was at the bookstore, they are having a local author book signing next Saturday."

"Oh really?"

"Yeah. I think he writes mystery and thrillers like you like."

"Huh. What his name? Did you catch it?"

"Um. Shoot. If you hadn't asked. Uh. Anthony something."

"Really?"

Emily places a finger to her bottom lip and searches the ceiling. "Gerald. Yeah, that's it. Anthony Gerald."

"Anthony Gerrald? No, I don't think I've heard of him. It'd be cool to check it out though."

"Yeah, I thought so too. I really liked that bookstore. It had such a cozy atmosphere. And the owners really made you feel at home."

"That's good. Yeah, let's plan to do it. Samuel would probably enjoy it too. Maybe we could go to the museum afterwards. I know that's something he's been wanting to do for a while now."

Emily snuggles up close to him and he places his arm around her. She nods her head and says, "Yeah. He'd liked that."

Eli kisses the top of her head before reaching over and turning out the lamp. Eli began to doze with a symphony of words playing through his mind. They had the same theme as the words he'd written down a few days before. They flowed through his mind and seeped deep into his soul. As the melody of words embraced him, sleep crept closer until he drifted off into the abyss.

†††

CAITLYNN FINDS HERSELF back at the tree overlooking the meadow. This time she is accompanied by both the angelic lady and Phil from the street. They are both adorned in spotless white garments and have a glimmering sheen to their complexions. They've told her someone is coming, and the visit is important. Her first thought was that it was her mother. Something had happened. Or it could be her grandpa.

As Caitlynn ponders her thoughts, she hears Phil say behind her, "Look. There he is." A jubilant joy radiates from his voice, and she can hear him smiling.

Caitlynn looks down towards the river and finds Eli standing there in awe and wonder. She hears him laughing as he spins around to take in all the beauty. She watches as he rushes over to the river and squats to gather a handful of water.

He gulps it down and continues laughing. Caitlynn watches as he turns his eyes to the tree where they stand. He rises and begins running towards them.

"What do I say?" Caitlynn asks nervously.

"Just say what's on your heart, my child," the lady says.

Eli conquers the hill and bends at the waist a few feet from them to catch his breath. He looks up at Caitlynn with his hands to his knees and says, "You're the one, aren't you?"

Caitlynn nods.

With his breath escaping him, Eli asks, "Why me? You were so young and had the rest of your life to live."

Caitlynn looks to the lady and Phil, then back to Eli. "It's not my place to question it, but I will not regret my decision as long as you continue to live in the present and cherish each day. Be where your feet are and don't waste a single day. Love your life and family like it could all be taken away tomorrow because it can. Do what makes you happy and never shy away from lending a helping hand. You've been given a second chance, so don't waste it."

She watches Eli's Adam's Apple take a long bob as he nods his head. "I can feel you, you know? It's like a part of you lives in me now. I'm different."

Caitlynn dips her head and says, "Good. That's good. May it always be a reminder for you. Lean into that and let my presence guide you. People need you, Eli. There's plenty of meanness going around in the world, and I think it could use a little more kindness. Love people and love your family."

Through a cracked voice, Eli manages to say, "I will," before the two embrace in a hug. They squeeze each other tight.

Caitlynn pulls back and says, "Can you do me a favor?"

"Sure, what's that?"

"Keep a check on my parents for me, okay? It's going to be tough on them this Christmas."

"Of course."

"And there's something I want you to give them."

Eli studies her as she takes hold of his hand and places a folded note into it.

"Remember these words and write them down. They will be important to my parents."

Eli nods.

A great wind swept through the meadow and began to climb its way towards the tree. Birds took to the air. Caitlynn hugged Eli again and whispered into his ear just before everything went dark.

11

When Eli awoke the next morning, the dream was fresh in his mind and so were the words written on the note that Caitlynn had given him. Eli stirred in bed and tossed the covers aside before Emily had risen.

"Honey, what's wrong? Are you okay?" she asked with a startle in her voice.

"I'm fine. I'm fine. I need something to write with. Do you have a pen and piece of paper in here?"

"Do what?" Emily asks with squinted eyes. "Why do you need that?"

"I had a dream last night about the girl that donated her heart. I think she gave me something she wants me to give to her family. I have to write it down before I forget."

Emily stares at him blankly before rubbing her face free of sleep.

"What? I'm serious," Eli says.

"You think she visited you or something?"

Eli pauses from searching in the nightstand drawers and nods.

Emily climbs out of bed and searches the nightstand on her side. "Here. You can use this, just make sure I get my pen back."

Eli takes the pen and paper and sits at the edge of the bed to write from memory of the dream.

Emily comes over and sits next to him. She places her arms around his shoulders and watches as he writes.

Eli shuts his eyes and searches his mind.

"It was so real and vivid. It's like I was really there. Everything was so beautiful. I can't even begin to try and describe it. It's like my mind was not capable of comprehending what I was seeing."

"Well, what *did* you see?"

"Heaven. It was heaven, Em. Oh my gosh was it gorgeous. There was this lush meadow with the greenest and plushest grass I've ever seen right next to this crystal-clear river that reflected mini rainbows when the sun hit it just right. There were all sorts of birds and other animals. The deer would walk right up to you and smell you without any fear. Then there was this huge live oak looking tree sitting up on a hill. It was the size of the tree of life in Lion King. Just humongous." Eli says the last part with a wide arc demonstration of his hands. "That's where I saw Caitlynn Richards. There was a man and woman with her. The man was the homeless man I bumped into before my heart attack." Eli swallows and looks at Emily, "I think he was an angel."

"My goodness."

"Then Caitlynn spoke to me and gave me a note with these words on them. They go along with what I had written down the other night. I've been having these moments where a string of words like from a poem or something will float before my minds eye and nag me all day until I write them down. I think she wants me to give it to her parents."

"Let me see."

Eli hands Emily what he'd written. She takes a few moments to read it. He watches tears fill her eyes as she places a hand over her mouth.

She finishes and looks at Eli.

"Honey, this is beautiful. Oh, my goodness. You have to share this with her family."

Eli nods. He and Emily embrace and hold each other for a good while.

A few hours later the Grindalls find themselves pulling into the driveway of the Richards family.

"Are you sure we should be doing this?" Eli asks Emily from the passenger seat as she shifts into park.

"Are you kidding? Of course. Whether they welcome our visit or not is up to them, but at least you know you did what you thought

Caitlynn wanted you to do. Besides, I'm sure they will be happy to see you."

Eli lets out a long breath and says, "Let's hope so." He turns and looks at Samuel in the back seat, "Things may get pretty emotional in there, but hang with us, okay? And be on your best behavior. Got it?"

Samuel nods a big nod as he fiddles with his Hulk figurine.

Moments later they reach the front porch.

Eli puts his head down and draws a deep breath. Emily rubs his back. Eli wipes his face and presses the Ring doorbell button. Seconds drag on for what feels like hours as they wait. Finally, footsteps can be heard coming to the door. Eli steps back and prepares himself. He watches the door swing open to reveal a middle-aged man with a salt and peppered beard dressed in khakis and a black zip up sweater. He had red, strained eyes behind his glasses either from liquor, tears, or both. Sleep looked like it had been hard to come by for the man. He studied Eli and his family as he stood in the opening with a hand on the door.

"What is this? Who are you?" the man asked.

Eli cleared his throat, "Hello. I'm uh. Well. I'm Eli Grindall. This is my wife, Emily. And my son, Samuel."

The man cranes his head, trying to place the importance of the name.

"Are you Dave Richards?"

Dave nods.

"You probably don't know who I am, but I am the man whose life your daughter saved."

With that, the blood drains from Dave's face and a shadow crosses over it. The man blinks and takes a step back. He looks at the floor and rubs his neck then looks back at Eli. He bites his inner lip and says, "The doctors mentioned something about you. They weren't sure if you would be an exact match or not. Heart or kidney?"

"Heart."

"They said they thought someone else in need of a kidney was a match. What happened to you?"

"I had a massive heart attack. I wouldn't be here if not for your daughter, Sir."

Dave tightens his lips and nods, "She was always a giver, that one. The most unselfish person I've ever known." Dave stares into the yard as tears moisten his eyes.

Samuel drops his Hulk toy and the sound of it hitting the ground brings Dave back.

He sniffles and says, "Please, come inside. Can I get you some coffee or tea to drink?"

"No. No. We're fine. Thank you though." Eli says after glancing at Emily who shakes her head.

Dave shuts the door behind them and calls out, "Hey Beth . . . we have company dear."

The home is a modest two-story single family on the outskirts of town. Nothing fancy. Likely built in the early two thousands and well kept through the years. It holds a unique, southern charm to it with all the hardwood floors and stained trim and hand railing to the stairs. A big, stained overhead beam separates the living area and kitchen. The place reminds Eli of something from that Fixer Upper show Emily likes to watch. The one with that Chip and Joanna couple. Seated on the couch with legs crossed and combing through a large photo album, is who Eli assumes to be Mrs. Richards. Or Beth as Dave had called her.

The lady looks up from the photos as they enter the room. She lowers her glasses and gives them a questioning look.

"Beth. This is Eli Grindall and his family."

Beth questions her husband with her eyes.

"Eli is a donor recipient."

Beth's eyes grow wide, and Eli watches her lips begin to tremble. She swallows hard and sets aside the photo album. Beth stands to greet them.

Eli shakes her hand and says, "It's a pleasure to meet you Mrs. Richards."

"Pardon my manners, I don't believe I properly introduced myself earlier," says Dave as he extends a hand to Eli and Emily. He squats and gets a high five from Samuel.

"No worries, Mr. Richards. I apologize for showing up unannounced like this. It's just I felt compelled to introduce myself."

"Non-sense. No need to apologize."

After taking their seats in the living area, Beth speaks up first, "I have to ask. What are you a recipient of?"

"Uh. Well. Um. I had a massive heart attack and ended up getting a life saving transplant at the last minute. The doctors say I am a miracle."

Beth stares at him without blinking before her eyes drift to his chest for a long moment.

Eli can feel his heart thumping hard against his ribs.

Ba-thump. Ba-thump. Ba-thump.

Beth bites her bottom lip and says, "My baby girl's in there."

Though her words were a bit strange, Eli understood perfectly what she meant.

Eli drew a deep breath before asking, "Would you like to listen to it beat?"

Dave and Beth draw closer to each other and squeeze each other's hands. They look at him blankly for a moment before looking into each other's eyes. Tears begin to flow before Beth looks back at Eli and says, "Please. It would mean so much."

Eli gives them a wink and says with a choked voice, "I thought so." He opens up his jacket and retrieves a stethoscope he'd bought at CVS on the way over.

He unbuttons his flannel shirt and hands Beth the stethoscope. Eli guides her hand to the right spot.

Ba-thump. Ba-thump. Ba-thump.

Beth gasps and covers her mouth.

"Oh, my sweet baby. Oh, Jesus."

Dave rubs her back and wipes his eyes.

Eli sniffles and wipes tears with the back of his hand. He hears Emily choking up beside him as she squeezes his hand. He glances over and sees even Samuel wiping at his eyes.

Beth pulls back and hands the stethoscope to her husband before disappearing into the kitchen.

Dave breaths deep and looks at the ceiling as he slides the device over Eli's/Caitlynn's heart.

Ba-thump. Ba-thump. Ba-thump.

Dave drops the stethoscope and covers a hand over his beard. He begins to weep. His shoulders hitch. He gulps for air. Snot flows. He stands to search for the Kleenexes. He finds them and offers some to Eli and Emily before excusing himself to tend to Beth in the kitchen.

Eli looks over at Emily and raises his eyebrows before blowing out a deep breath. Emily leans into his side and he kisses her.

After a few moments, Dave and Beth reenter the room.

"Sorry about that," Beth says.

Eli waves her off with both hands and says, "Please, no need. We totally understand."

The couple sits back down across from them.

As Beth dabs at her eyes, she says, "It's just been so hard. It was so unexpected. She was so healthy and full of life . . ." She trails off at the end as if catching herself on something. She shakes her head and adds, "At least we thought."

Eli arches his brows.

"Apparently on the day of the accident, she'd received a call from the doctor. She was diagnosed with stage three colon cancer just moments before. We had no idea. She never said anything about having issues or nothing."

"Oh, my goodness," Emily says.

"She was given three years to live. Five, if all of her treatments went perfectly well. Then, bam. All this happened."

"I'm so sorry," Eli says.

Dave crosses his arms, smiles, and leans back, "But you know, she would have been so thrilled to know she was able to help you and all the others. She really did just love people. She'd give you the shirt off her back without even thinking about it. It was just who she was."

Eli remembers how meek and kind she seemed in the dream last night. Dave's words are of no surprise.

Beth smiles and chimes in, "And boy did she love animals. Oh, my gosh. Her dream was to open her own veterinarian clinic one day. That's what she was going to school for."

"Really? How about that," Emily says.

"I found her diary last week. I've been reading it every day and every night before bed. All she talks about in it is wanting to leave behind a legacy and how she wants to help people and love on people. She talks about leaving her mark and how there's plenty of meanness going around in the world, and that it could always use a little more kindness. I want to frame that phrase one day." Beth smiles and looks out the window.

That phrase resonates with Eli as he recalls the dream and Caitlynn saying those exact words. A chill runs down Eli's spine as gooseflesh covers his body. He digs in his breast pocket and retrieves a folded piece of paper.

He clears his throat and says, "I had a dream last night. It's a dream that I will remember for as long as I live." Eli has to fight back the tears, "I saw Caitlynn in it, and she said those same words to me. Then she gave me a folded note that had these words on it."

Eli studies the words for a moment before handing the paper to Beth. The words read:

So fragile life is. Here and gone in a flash.
We never know when death may call,

Randall Lane

So make the most out of your little dash.

A choice must now be made,
To be bitter for a life taken too soon?
Or to be grateful for the time you had.

Cherish those around you.
Family, Friends, and Pets because they
May not be here tomorrow.

Live each day like it's your last.
For just when you think it's safe,
It can all change in a flash.

Tomorrow is never promised to anyone.
We are all just a breath away from eternity.
Live so there are no regrets when life is done.

May we learn to be where our feet are.
Never too busy to lend a helping hand,
And to show the good side of the human heart.

Death is a journey we all must make alone.
Regardless of how hard it may be,
For it is but our first step towards home.

Beth looks at the words then looks up at Eli with wide eyes. He watches her take a gulp.

"You wrote this?"

Eli nods.

Beth hands the paper to Dave. He reads for a few moments then looks up at Eli in bewilderment.

Eli looks at them both with questioning eyes, "What's the matter?"

Dave sniffles and says, "This is the same poem that was found in her car."

All the air in the room is sucked out. A wave of chills is doused over him. Eli's breath ceases in his chest. He blinks at them. Emily squeezes his hand. He looks at her and she nods.

Eli clears his throat and tells them of everything in his dream.

Beth and Dave smile and cry as Eli recalls his little visit to Heaven and everything Caitlynn told him.

When Eli finishes, he looks out the window and watches the wind play with the leaves. Birds flutter and hop about the yard. Then a red cardinal lights on the window seal and looks in at them.

Eli smiles.

Beth follows his eyes to the bird and says, "Yeah, he stays there on the window seal. Every morning I find him sitting right there. All through the day we'll see him. He loves to sing and keep us company. Caitlynn loved cardinals growing up. They were always her favorite. I like to think it's her way of watching over us."

Eli nods, "Me too. Me too."

The cardinal looks in one last time then flies away to be carried with the wind.

12

Christmas Day
9 am

As the Richards family is gathered in the living room, Dave, Beth, the grandparents and aunts and uncles, Caitlynn is right there with them taking it all in. Her mother has Frank Sinatra playing through her small portable Victrola. He currently sings *Silent Night.* Candles burn throughout the home and the aroma of Cinnamon and Peppermint hangs heavy in the air. A makeshift memorial of sorts is stationed next to the Christmas tree. Photos of Caitlynn are sandwiched between candles and lighted glass angels. A slide show of Caitlynn's life is on the TV. The family sits close together and laughs and cries as the photos interchange. Caitlynn sits next to her parents and laughs and cries with them. She rubs her mom's back and smiles at the sight of her family drawing together.

Caitlynn sighs and turns to look out the window behind them. Standing beneath a Crape Myrtle is Phil and the angelic lady dressed in their white gowns. She hears the lady's voice in her spirit say, "We should be going before much longer, my child."

Just a little longer? Please?

She watches the lady look at Phil. The two smile and nod at Caitlynn.

Caitlynn has a feeling she'll be making that request a lot to those two.

It's so good to see her parents leaning on each other through all of this. She was so afraid they would drift further apart with her death but seeing them really rely on each other has brought such peace and joy to her spirit. With enough time and her frequent visits, she hopes things will be okay between them.

She turns from looking at Phil and the lady to look at her mom and dad. Her dad has his arm around her mom and is squeezing her tight as she leans into his side.

Caitlynn smiles.

Yeah. Things are going to be okay. She'll make sure of it.

†††

ELI AND EMILY TIPTOE down the hall to Samuel's room. The door is slightly cracked so Eli gives it a gentle push. As it opens, he and Emily find Samuel still asleep in his Batman pajamas. Shadow and Sunny, his two huskie puppies, are sleeping in their little beds on the floor beside Samuel's bed. He'd named them that because one is mostly black with some white tossed here and there and the other is all white except for some red and black near its face. The dogs perk up when they hear Eli and Emily. Eli walks over and sits on the side of Samuel's bed. He pats his son's leg and says with a big grin, "Time to wake up boy. You got work to do. Them presents ain't gonna unwrap themselves."

Samuel stirs and stretches, mumbling something Eli couldn't understand. Eli chuckles and ruffles Samuel's hair.

Samuel flashes open his eyes and blurts, "Presents! Did Santa come? Did Santa come?"

Eli stands and he and Emily laugh at the sight of Samuel rushing out of the room with Shadow and Sunny right on his heels. With his socked feet, Samuel skids into the living room. Eli hears him gasp at the sight of the overflow of gifts beneath the tree. Samuel turns around and looks at Eli and Emily with his jaw almost touching the floor.

"Are all those mine?"

"You betcha, Kiddo," Eli says with a smile as he hugs Emily tight against his ribs. "Well, don't just stand there, get to it."

Samuel crashes to the floor and goes to town. Eli and Emily take a seat on the couch and watch. A Christmas Story plays on the TV for the dozenth time since last night.

Sunny ambles over and takes a mouthful of wrapping paper and begins to tug on one of Samuel's presents.

"Good boy. There you go. Keep pulling. You almost have it," Samuel says with laughter pouring out of him.

Emily laughs and says, "My goodness, Sunny's going to open the whole thing."

"He sure is," Eli adds.

They spend the next ten minutes or so laughing with Samuel as he and the dogs open presents.

Emily elbows Eli's side. He turns to find her holding a small box wrapped in red paper with big Santa faces. Eli arches his brows at her.

"Go on open it," Emily says.

"Well, hold on. Let me get yours."

Eli stands and picks up a gift from beneath the tree. "Here you go."

Emily gives it a gentle shake and puts her ear to it. "Let me guess. A box full of rocks from the yard. Or wait that was supposed to be yours."

"Haha. Very funny," Eli says as he watches her begin to open it.

Emily balls up the paper and gets down to the black jewelry box. She squints her eyes at it and looks at Eli with a funny face.

He chuckles and says, "Go on. Open it up."

She does and says, "Awe," drawing out the word. Emily places a hand on her heart and says, "Eli. Oh, my goodness."

It's a necklace with a locket. On the front is an engraving from a photo booth picture they had taken on one of their first dates. Below them are the words, *I'm gonna love you…* The words to the Randy Travis song that Eli had played at their wedding.

"You have to see what's inside."

Emily opens the locket. Tears fill her eyes, and she wraps her arms around Eli's neck. Inside is a photo of an old man and woman sitting on a bench watching the sunset. Below the photo are the rest of the lyrics, *Forever and ever. Forever and ever, Amen.*

He and Emily hold each other for a good while before finishing with a passionate kiss.

It isn't long before Samuel hears and says, "Really? C'mon."

Eli and Emily chuckle like school kids. Eli reaches behind his shirt and pulls out a locket of his own.

"I have one just like it. I want it to be a reminder of the love and passion we had when we first fell in love. And it's my promise just like from our wedding day that I'm gonna love you forever and ever. Amen."

Emily hugs him again and gives him a quick kiss. She pulls back and wipes her eyes with the sleeve of her shirt before saying, "You still have to open yours."

"Oh," Eli smiles and starts opening.

Like the gift he'd gotten Emily, his is in a black jewelry box also.

"Don't tell me you got a necklace too."

"No. Not quite."

Eli opens the box to find a silver bracelet with a placard in the center. On the front is a picture of a cardinal in midflight. On the back side are the engraved words:

May we learn to be where our feet are.

Never too busy to lend a helping hand,

And to show the good side of the human heart.

"Oh babe," Eli says before they hug and kiss again.

Samuel stands to his feet and puts his hands to his hips. He charges Eli and the two begin to wrestle and laugh.

"Easy now," Emily says.

Shadow and Sunny bark at the commotion as they've already learned their protective instinct to watch over Samuel.

Eli wraps Samuel in his arms and squeezes him tight before planting a wet kiss on his cheek. "I love you boy."

"Love you too, Dad."

"C'mon. Time for a group hug," Eli says as he reaches over and pulls Emily into them.

Eli squeezes them for a good moment and kisses each of their heads.

"I love you both, so so much."

On the TV, little Ralphie had just discovered his Red Rider BB gun tucked behind the tree and is busy opening it as the old man looks on with joy.

†††

Saturday
December 30th

AFTER FINALLY FINDING a parking spot, the Grindalls exit their car and begin the trek to the bookstore in downtown Yawnoc. Anthony Gerald's book signing starts at noon and it's now twenty minutes till.

Samuel holds Eli and Emily's hands as they cross the intersection after waiting a few minutes for the light to change. The town is still decorated and playing Christmas music over outdoor speakers as if it'd just turned December 1st. Eli sips on a cup of coffee. Three creams and two sugars just the way he has come to like it. A horse drawn carriage rides in the road next to them. Samuel tries imitating the clopping sound of their feet on the pavement with heavy thumps of his own. Eli smiles then looks ahead towards the bookstore. In the sea of people, just in front of Ned's Diner, Eli thinks for a mere second, he gets a glimpse of Phil. He blinks to find it is a much younger man who is dressed similar to how Phil dressed. He doesn't hold a sign like Phil, but he does have a cup that he rattles at the people passing by.

The Grindalls reach the man and Eli stops.

Eli looks the man up and down, searching to see if it's Phil in disguise. Finally, Eli clears his throat and asks, "Care for a coffee and sandwich?"

The man licks his lips and says, "Sir, you have no idea."

"Wait right here. We'll be back, okay?"

"God bless you Sir. God bless you."

Eli takes Emily and Samuel inside Ned's Diner. As they stride up to the counter, Emily says into his ear, "Is that the man from your dreams?"

Eli shakes his head and grins, "I don't think so, but then again, Phil can be sneaky. Either way, the man looks hungry, wouldn't you say?"

"Most definitely."

Eli steps up to the register and places his order to a teenage boy with two black eyes and a broken arm.

"Geeze kid. Did you pick a fight with a grizzly bear?"

The boy looks at him and shakes his head, "Car wreck."

Eli felt his heart knock.

"Car wreck?"

The kid nods, "Will this be all?"

Eli swallows the knot in his throat and says, "Uh, yeah. Sure. Unless . . ." he turns to Emily and Samuel, "Did y'all want anything?" They both shake their heads.

The kid gives the total and takes Eli's payment. The whole time Eli is dying to ask the question. He decides against prodding too far. If this is the kid that killed Caitlynn Richards, he's probably been questioned enough already. Eli gets the coffee and sandwich, places a ten-dollar tip into the jar, and wishes the kid a quick recovery.

On the way out, Emily whispers, "Are you thinking what I'm thinking?"

"Yup. That was the guy."

"Lord have mercy," Emily says.

Eli finds the homeless man and gives him the order.

"Thank you so much, Sir. God Bless you."

"You're welcome. Come by the soup kitchen on 21st avenue, we'll be sure you're taken care of. Alright man?"

"Yeah okay. I'll do that. Thank you."

Eli smiles and pats the man on the shoulder before turning towards the bookstore. Once there, Eli glances back towards Ned's to look for the man. He stares through the crowd of people but doesn't see him. Wait. There. It looks like Phil. Eli blinks and squints. He's gone.

Samuel tugs on his hand and gets his attention. A man and woman had just exited the bookstore and the man stood holding the door for them. As Eli steps closer, he catches glimpse of his reflection in the glass. Except it wasn't his reflection at all. It was Caitlynn's. She stands there with her golden locks of hair dangled over a black peacoat with a black wool beanie pulled down tight just above her bright green eyes. She smiles and dips her head.

Eli returns her gesture and says, "I see ya girl. You'll always be with me, won't ya?"

He thanks the man holding the door then steps inside and finds a seat to listen in on this Anthony Gerald fella.

Thank you for reading *A Christmas Spirit!* I hope you enjoyed it as much as I did writing it! If so, I would be grateful if you'd be kind enough to leave a review on Amazon as reviews truly are the life blood of any Author's career.

About the Author

I am a former college baseball player turned writer who thoroughly enjoys the outdoors, whether it be fishing, kayaking, hiking, and exploring new places, or watching a game of America's greatest pastime. I'm an old soul at heart, so I love old music (especially classic rock from CCR, Bob Seger, Bruce Springsteen, or vintage rock and roll from Chuck Berry, Muddy Water's, Elvis, etc. I also love me some Hank Williams, Johnny Cash, Waylon Jennings, Randy Travis, and the like) old movies and antique items. I own a Victrola Turntable in case you're not getting the picture yet.

I'm an avid reader and writer of Mystery, Horror, and Suspense. I enjoy reading Stephen King, Ted Dekker, Frank Peretti, Thomas Harris, Steven James, C.J. Box, and James Lee Burke to name a few. I also enjoy a fun/inspiring Southern Story as well such as Where the Crawdads Sing. I was a top ten finalist in Inkshares Mystery/Thriller and Horror contests. I am a member of both the Horror Writers Association and Mystery Writers of America.

I hold an MBA from Coastal Carolina University and am currently practicing real estate in Myrtle Beach. You can find me on Instagram, Facebook, and YouTube to stay up to date with my latest work.

You can find me on Instagram, Facebook, and YouTube to stay up to date with my latest work.
>
Instagram: randall_lane31
Facebook: Randall Lane Fiction
YouTube: Randall Lane Fiction
Amazon: Randall Lane Fiction

Other Books Available

If you enjoyed *A Christmas Spirit* then you'll likely enjoy my latest novel *The Reaping* as well. Available on Amazon! The book trailer is posted to my YouTube channel.

Synopsis: Something strange is happening in New England. Over the past 17 years, numerous children have disappeared after each of their parents were discovered brutally murdered and left with taunting notes. With rumors of the man in a black hood who roams the woods at night, to an escaped mental patient from Cushing Island, and a snake handling church with a dark past, veteran Homicide Detective, Laurie Daniels must work through this high stakes enigma to learn who the ghost-like killer really is. The deeper she goes the more she begins to believe the killer may be connected to her past. And a new, horrifying clue emerges . . . Daniels isn't closing in on the killer, but he's closing in on her. Can she catch him before he catches her?

My other novel *Devil's Den* is available as well. The book trailer is posted to my YouTube channel.

Synopsis: The year is 1989 and as Detectives search for a local serial killer, James and Rebecca Randolph can't help but wonder if it may be Ethan, the new co-worker of James. After causing a horrendous accident at the Georgetown International Paper Mill, Ethan vanishes before further questioning. Locals are quick to term him the GTK or Georgetown Killer. 25 years later, after relocating to Holden Beach, James and Rebecca find themselves once again in the cross hairs of the GTK. As they consult the spiritual guidance of Native American Friends, they soon learn there is a lot more going on than meets the eye. Embarking on a Journey from Darkness to Light, passing through the Devil's Den along the way, they gain a whole new perspective of the saying, "Good vs Evil."

I also have my novel *Omah*, available on Amazon too! To watch the book trailer, head over to my YouTube channel. (Randall Lane Fiction.)

Synopsis: After a string of mysterious disappearances and encounters in Northern California, Game Wardens are less than surprised when six-year-old Tyler Jacob's vanishes by the South Fork Eel River while fishing with his family. As the family is riddled with guilt and on the verge of losing hope, Native Americans from the local Yurok Tribe step in to help spread light on the recent events. While pushing through the vast wilderness and majestic Redwood Forest in search of his son, Randy Jacob's soon learns that what he once thought was just a Legend may actually be a living and breathing creature after all. As hours stretch into days and the clock rushes forward, can Tyler be found before it's too late?

Be sure to check out my collection of short stories titled, *Night Terrors!*

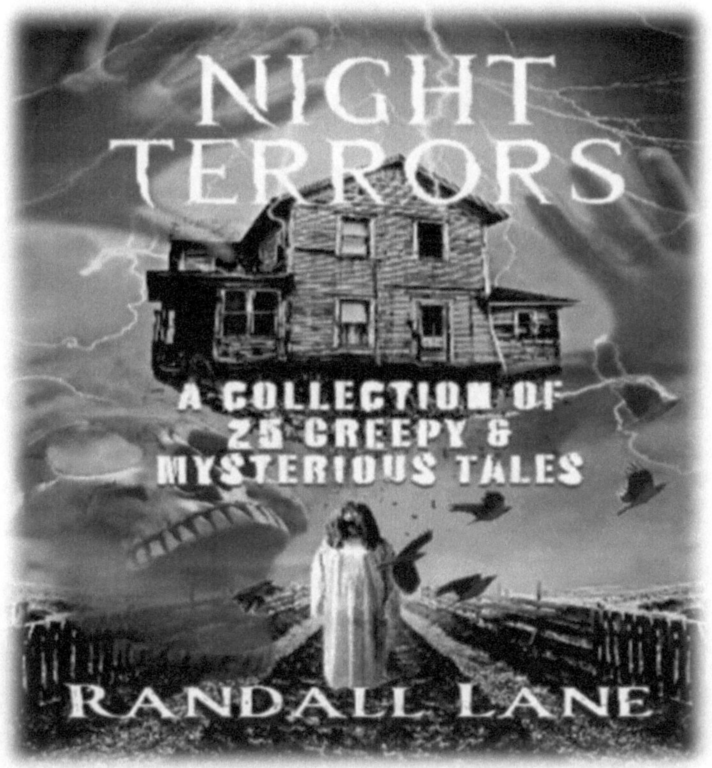

INCLUDES EVERYTHING FROM GHOSTS, ALIENS, BIGFOOT, WEREWOLVES, SKINWALKERS, STRANGE DISAPPEARANCES, AND MANY OTHER CREEPY MYSTERIES.

A Christmas Spirit
Inside Look at Chapter 1

of Randall's next Novel

OLD
GHOSTS
OF THE
VALLEY

A NOVEL

RANDALL LANE

1

Chapel Valley, NC

October 2023

3:33 p.m.

Carol Gore is a fifty-nine-year-old divorced mother of two, who lives alone up in the backcountry of the Blue Ridge Mountains. She has lived in the same house since the early nineties. She and her husband, Steve, moved to the area after he'd picked up a mining job in the town of Chapel Valley. It was also around this time that Carol learned of the Abbott cult. A co-worker from Piggly Wiggly wouldn't shut up about the sweet little Abbott family and its parishioners, so Carol finally relented and accompanied her to an event at the compound. That was all it took for Carol to become hooked.

As Carol thinks back to the moment she first stepped foot on the Abbott compound, she subconsciously rinses off a few glass plates from previous days meals. Skylar, her white Himalayan cat, is busy weaving in and out between her feet. The tickle brings her back just in time to hear the strange noise. Carol thought she'd heard something earlier but only brushed it off as a play upon her ears. Must be the house settling or something, she'd said to herself. Isn't that what we always say? Or at least what we always hope for, right? What if we're wrong though? What if we're not alone during all the times we think we are? What if someone or something . . . lurks within the shadows and watches without our knowing?

As Carol asks herself these questions, she hears it again. The sound is unmistakable this time. The creaking of a floorboard beneath a sturdy, unwelcomed foot. All day she had fought the eerie feeling of being watched. It seems a presence had been hovering just over her shoulder. She's being too paranoid, she'd thought. Things are different now. To think she's still being watched . . . well it'll just end up driving her crazy. She can't allow herself to go on thinking this way. They would end up throwing her away to the place where people drift along in white gowns, while being force fed medicine and whipped into submission. She'll never go back there. She'd made a promise to herself, and she's determined within her heart to keep it.

No amount of self-encouragement can eat away the growing feeling she has of being watched. It is stronger now than ever before. The home is quiet other than the running of the faucet, and the black and white film playing in the living room. Carol stands frozen with her back to the rest of the kitchen. She looks down to find Skylar staring behind her. Together they listen.

Creeeaaak!

Skylar hisses and enters in a low crouch, his ears flare backward, his hair stands straight. Carol feels someone in the room. She turns just enough, so she can scan the room with her peripheral. She goes over the China cabinet full of Grandma's dishes and scans over the kitchen table. Her heart leaps at the big shadow of a man standing in the kitchen's door frame. She gasps and drops a dish. The crash of the shattering glass fills the room. She fights the urge to look directly at the man, knowing that the chance of her survival will quickly diminish should she see his face.

Skylar emits a low growl and backs up to be between Carol and the sink cabinet.

"What do you want?" Carol asks with her words sticking to her throat.

A moment passes.

"You."

Creeeeaaaaak!

The dark man takes a step.

"Stop. Don't come any closer."

He stops.

She grips the sinks hard enough to hurt her fingers.

"Look at me."

She shakes her head.

"Carol."

Her heart sinks at the knowledge of this mystery man knowing her name.

"Carol. You have to look at me. It's very important."

She clamps her eyes shut and shakes her head again.

She hears him breathe deep. He holds it, then sighs.

"I don't want to do this Carol, but I'm afraid I have to. You're leaving me no—"

Carol snatches Skylar up and bolts through the side door of the kitchen for her bedroom. Heavy thuds pound towards her. She slams the door shut and engages the lock. She rushes to move a chest of drawers against the door.

The dark man slams against the door as soon as Carol slides the furniture into place. The door rattles hard on its hinges. She stumbles backwards with one hand to her mouth, and the other reaching blindly for the bed.

Her heart will surely explode any moment as adrenaline courses through her veins in an icy rush. Her legs meet the edge of the bed, and she bruises a heel against the metal railing below. She winces and bends to tend to the pain.

The door rattles hard once more. Skylar growls again before going into a frantic search for cover. Another hard thud pounds against the door.

As Carol rubs her heel, she begins to hear a faint but hoarse whisper coming from under the bed. The scratchy voice stalls her racing heart and sends her body freezing in place. Movement comes from beneath the bed. It sounds like something crawling across the hardwood floor. Carol jerks herself up and looks toward the window. A sudden thought hits her. What an idiot. Last week she'd nailed the windows shut after fearing someone was secretly entering in the night. In her efforts to keep someone out, she ends up trapping herself in. She must break it. She races over to a nightstand and begins to search for something to break the glass.

The whisper under the bed becomes more audible now. Between the thuds against the door, she can make out the words. It's saying, "Come near my dear."

Carol yanks open a drawer to her nightstand and pulls out a hammer she's used for hanging pictures. She tucks her face into the crevice of her elbow and takes a swing. The window shatters. She rakes away the shards along the seal and rushes over to the nightstand. As she begins to swipe away the clutter, lamp and all, the thing beneath the bed growls loudly. Carol catches a glimpse in her peripheral of a long, bony hand reaching out from beneath the bed, aiming for Carol's ankle. She screams and jumps backwards. The thing continues to growl. Its pale fingers fall limp to the hardwood. Its nails make a loud tapping sound.

Carol hurries and places the nightstand beneath the broken window. The door thuds again as she climbs upon the nightstand.

She wiggles through the window and falls to the ground. Her hip barks in protest. She grunts and manages to get to her feet. She hears her bedroom door burst open. She doesn't turn back to look but makes a break for the grove of pines.

Running and stumbling her way into the tree line, she pushes away the swipes of bony branches. Her tender feet scream with every poke and jab from the sticks and pine needles. Her lungs burn like they've been doused with gasoline and lit to a flame. Her breath steams into the frigid air. Running between the pines, she retrieves her cell. Moments later she finds the contact she's looking for and places the call.

Panting and glancing over her shoulder, she waits for her son to answer.

Tales from Uncle Joe
MUTILATIONS
RANDALL LANE

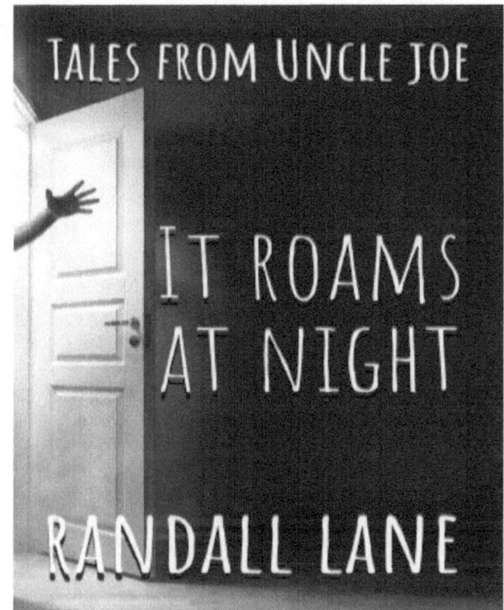

Tales from Uncle Joe
IT ROAMS AT NIGHT
RANDALL LANE

Tales from Uncle Joe
AN INSIDE JOB
RANDALL LANE

Thank you once again for joining me on this journey through story. From one reader to another, may we all continue to find ourselves as we escape into the written word.

Till next time!

All the best,

Randall Lane